PASADENA

PASADENA

SHERRI L. SMITH

G. P. PUTNAM'S SONS

G. P. PUTNAM'S SONS
an imprint of Penguin Random House LLC
375 Hudson Street
New York, NY 10014

Copyright © 2016 by Sherri L. Smith.

G. P. Putnam's Sons is a registered trademark of Penguin Random House LLC.

Library of Congress Cataloging-in-Publication Data is available upon request.
Printed in the United States of America.
ISBN 978-1-101-99625-6

10 9 8 7 6 5 4 3 2 1

Design by Annie Ericsson.
Text set in New Caledonia LT Std.

For Kelvin—

It would be a bitter little world without you.

1

Maggie always was a fucking train wreck. Leave it to her to end up facedown in a swimming pool on the hottest day of summer.

Caller ID shows Joey called five times. The sixth time, he left a message. I played it once, the phone close to my ear, then listened to the echo of my own breathing over the open line, waiting for his words to sink in. When they did, I hung up.

"I have to go home."

"What?" Danielle says. We're at a diner in Cape May on the Jersey Shore. My cousin shovels a handful of fried clam strips into her face. "We just got here," she says, her mouth stuffed. It's disgusting.

I turn and look out the window. Summer rain dots the plate glass, turning the trees along the side of the road into watercolor. Across the street, well-tended Victorian houses staunchly ignore the shower as tourists run by in flip-flops and canopied bicycle surreys.

It's my first time back to see family since my mother and I moved out west. I thought I'd been missing the East Coast, but there's a sour feeling in my stomach, one I haven't felt since the last time I was here.

We'd gone to California to be new people, to have a fresh start. But bad things happen everywhere. Even in the land of sun and roses.

That's why I left for the summer. And that's why I'm going back again.

I shake my head, annoyed at Dani after the thunderclap of bad news. "Not *your* home. Mine."

Dani's dark lashes flutter and her eyes go wide. "Back to LA?"

My cousin loves the thought of it—Hollywood, Los Angeles. She resents me for being here when we could have both been back there for the summer. But I don't live in LA, her fabled City of Angels. I live on the outskirts, in Pasadena.

I shut the phone in my hand, pressing it to my cheek

like an ice pack that can stop the pounding in my head. "Maggie's dead."

Dani's mouth forms a perfect O of stupidity. "Your BFF?"

"That's the one."

Dani's face turns a shade of gray. "Oh, Jude, that's awful. What happened?"

I don't answer because I don't know.

Dani waits, clears her throat. Then she starts in on her French fries.

I unlock my phone and call the airline, avoiding the text messages in the open window, the ones that Maggie would never respond to now.

I turn back to the scene out the window, pressing buttons in the voice mail tree to book my flight. The rain, the incessant greenery feels flamboyant next to my memory of California. Water streams down the window, tracing shadows on my skin like the promise of tears. Three hundred fifty dollars is the cost of changing my summer plans. The cover charge for the suicide of my best friend. I stifle a laugh, and feel a hole opening up inside me. Maggie's gone.

But why?

There must be a reason.

That's what I tell myself the entire ride to the airport.

Strung out on too much adult sympathy and not enough sleep, I try to drum logic into my head.

My aunt and cousin drop me at the terminal with its forced air and forced smiles. They don't give gifts or linger. No cash in the palm, or saltwater taffy. I've tainted their perfect summer.

When I hand the airline rep my bereavement-rate ticket, he realizes I'm a minor traveling alone and I get special treatment. At seventeen, they don't give me any cheap plastic wings. Just a seat against the bulkhead, where the flight attendants can keep an eye on me, and a Diet Coke before takeoff.

I tell myself that I haven't had time to call Joey. Not between packing and travel. He would know what really happened. Joey's good at that. Knowing. Except for when it comes to him and me. Besides, I don't want to know just yet. Details are pedestrian when it comes to suicide—overdose, razor blade, gunshot, asphyxiation. There are only so many ways to off yourself. It's not really the *how* that matters anyway, just the who, the what, and the why.

The who is Maggie. Drop-dead gorgeous Maggie Kim.

The last time I saw her out by the pool, she was dressed like a movie star—black one-piece suit, strapless, the same thick ebony as her glossy bob of hair. Big round sunglasses that would have made me look like a bug, but looked elegant on her. She'd worn a sheer black robe over it all, and candy-apple-red patent leather mules that clacked loudly on the pebbled surface of the deck but matched the polish on her manicure and toes.

She'd held a cigarette between perfectly painted lips, one of those nasty little filterless things that she loved so much she'd order them online by the boxful. You'd have thought it was a brick of heroin, the way she clung to the box when the UPS delivery came.

I tried one once, when she wasn't looking. Me, the Goody Two-shoes, the Sandra Dee. I didn't even light it. The taste of tobacco on my lips was enough to make me puke.

She caught me hunched over the toilet and smiled with those professionally pearly whites, so striking against her red lips and almond-brown skin. "Don't mess with Mommy's candy," she'd told me. Then she'd laughed and held my hair, even though it was already in a ponytail.

Poor Maggie.

I failed her.

Between the complimentary drink service and the meal cart, I finally break down and cry.

2

California rises up to meet me. The jet wheels hit the tarmac with a 2.5 Richter rumble.

Home. It's so bright out here, so the opposite of my green summer getaway.

I dig into my bag for sunglasses and come up empty. In a flash, I can see them, three thousand miles away, lying on my borrowed bed. Figures. I squint and make my way to the cabstand.

When the 101 Freeway gives way to the 134, my pulse quickens. We speed through Glendale and Eagle Rock, the smudgy soup bowl of Downtown LA spread out to my right. The hillside on my left is blasted, the golden-brown grass singed to a blackened streak of a cigarette-caused wildfire that probably shut down traffic for most of rush hour. I lower my window and try to smell the smoke, but it's long gone, eradicated by LA's finest. I close the window. It's almost good to be home.

Almost.

And then we're at Orange Grove, peeling off the freeway to the south, and a lump the size of a lemon hits my throat. "Stop here," I say as we reach Colorado Boulevard and the stretch of stores crowding the street with tourists and locals alike. I pay the man and find a store with a sunglass stand for the unprepared. Sunblock and hats fill the back of the rack. In February, it'll be ponchos and umbrellas.

I buy two pairs of cheap glasses. Not fashionable, but at least they hide my red eyes.

Big girls don't cry, Maggie used to say. They get even.

Joey answers his phone before the first ring ends. "Joe, I'm back. I'm at the Coffee Bean on Fair Oaks. Come get me?"

I didn't even have to ask. I heard his car keys the minute he said hello. He's got a special ringtone for me. Everyone used to tease me about it. A song from an old movie. Supposed to be romantic, but I've never seen it.

• • •

"Welcome back," Joey says, bumping into an empty chair in his rush to greet me.

I'm in the back of the coffeehouse, away from the picture windows and the summer crowds, at a small wooden table for two. I take my feet off the extra chair, put down my iced coffee, and let him pull me into a hug. It's awkward and lasts too long for my comfort, but I figure he needs it. He deserves it. Joey's the one who found Maggie's body.

He wraps his arms around my bare shoulders and clings to me, smelling of fabric softener and boy sweat.

"Jude, it was awful. I—"

That lump in my throat is getting bigger. "Not here, Joey. Not yet." My eyes ache. It would be a mistake to cry in front of him. A cliché, one he'd be quick to embrace. I shake my head, my voice barely a whisper. "In the car, okay?"

"Sorry," he says, pulling away. His fingers leave my skin reluctantly. I shrug and take in his gangly figure, shredded jeans, and the ever-present unbuttoned shirt over a plain white tee. This is Joey's uniform. Only the state of the jeans and the color of the shirt changes. It's reliable, like him.

"Thanks for coming to get me."

"Sure, no problem." Suddenly, he's all elbows and shy glances, no longer looking at me directly. He's gotten taller since school ended. Not a great development for a kid who already looked like a young giraffe.

"This your bag?" he asks, reaching for my pink-and-purple duffel. I don't answer, just grab my matching backpack and follow him out the door.

"Did you want a drink or something?" I ask belatedly. "My treat."

"Not now, thanks. I just hit Jamba Juice before you called." He pats his nonexistent stomach and swings my bag over his shoulder.

"Sorry I'm parked so far away," he says as we head south, away from the shopping area. "The lot was full and parking is a bitch around here on a Sunday."

"Yeah." I suck the last of my drink dry and roll the sweating plastic cup against my cheek. It's oven-hot today, and the city smells like a dozen little grass fires waiting to happen.

"Here we are," Joey says, tweaking the unlock button on his car key. A silver ZX convertible bleats in response. The top is down to protect it from being sliced by stereo thieves. Radios are cheap. Soft tops are not. Joey tosses my bag in the back and we climb in.

I kick off my clogs and put my feet on the dashboard. Joey pulls an old paperback out of my way and drops it in the backseat.

Maggie used to do this—take her shoes off in the car. Even in winter. She drove barefoot too. Said she could feel the road better that way.

I feel five hours of airplane cramps and a knot in my stomach.

There are reasons I went away for the summer. But now I'm back. Still, there's no need to head home. Not just yet.

"Can we go to Maggie's?" I ask. "I should see her parents."

"Sure," Joey says. And like the good boy he is, he drives in silence, radio off, and lets me gather my thoughts.

We drive down along the arroyo, big houses looking confused at the passing of the century. Craftsman mansions and stone monoliths that look like scattered university buildings rather than private homes. Oaks and magnolias shade the curving boulevards with names like characters from Fitzgerald novels. I read them as they go by.

The magnolia trees are in bloom and the air is alive with the thick scent of flowers and pollen. Joey's car is dusted in yellow granules that blow past us as we drive. I take a deep breath, drawing summer into my lungs. "Okay," I say. "Tell me."

Joey wipes his nose, clears his throat, and sniffs. He keeps one hand on the wheel and his eyes on the road. "I don't know. I just. I hadn't seen her in a couple of days, but we were supposed to catch a matinee. We had talked about it at Dane's birthday party. I took the side gate, came around the corner of the house, and there she was. Floating. But not facedown like in the movies. She was looking up, with the sun on her face. I thought she was swimming, but she didn't move, she didn't answer when I said her name. I jumped in, pulled her out, tried to get her breathing, but it didn't help. I screamed until her father came to the back door. He called 9-1-1."

I listen to Joey recount the details of my best friend's death, how she looked, how the pool was cold. How her lips were tinged with blue.

I revise the image in my mind: Maggie, faceup, staring at the sky. Estimated time of death: 11:00 p.m. He tells me the paramedics called the coroner's office. How there was an autopsy, rushed because the coroner knew the family. Mr. Kim is a somebody in Pasadena.

It's likely the Kims panicked out of concern for their

son, Parker. He "isn't well," as the understatement goes. The slightest hint of danger to his health, and he gets whisked away to a roomful of doctors. If Maggie had died of anything contagious, they'd want to know. Their little boy has been dying slowly for so long, heaven forbid something like swine flu come along and kill him overnight.

But it wasn't swine flu.

We reach Maggie's street, a wide treeless avenue except for a few ridiculously tall palms, the kind that are deadly in high winds with their razor-blade sheaves flying like weighted boomerangs. No fruit, no flowers, and not a lick of shade. They're wealthy trees, arrogant and useless. They remind me of Maggie's parents.

"It was an accident," I say as we make the turn. The block is silent except for the ticking heat-click of air conditioners and the hum of the car. Maggie had called me before, threatening to kill herself. That's how I know she would never follow through. She loved the drama, and drama needs an audience. "It was an accident," I say again.

Joey doesn't look at me. "The coroner said suicide."

I take a deep breath. "Why? What did he find?"

He stays silent a moment. "They're still running tests."

I lean forward, as if I can intimidate him into answering me. "Tests. On what?"

Joey shakes his head, as if he still can't believe it. "A bellyful of drugs."

"Violetta," I say by way of greeting when the home health aide answers the door. Parker must be back home from wheelchair camp if Violetta's here. Maggie's inoperable-tumor-filled brother is smart as a whip. He bites like one too. I used to think he was cute, when I was young enough to mistake sarcasm for flirting. I outgrew it.

"Mrs. Kim is in the garden," Violetta says. She holds the door open for me and Joey, then runs back upstairs. There's an elevator in the kitchen, but I guess that's for private use only. They treat Violetta like a butler, but she draws some of her own lines.

The house is hot. The Kims are rich enough to be stingy about things like climate control. Mr. Kim drives a ten-year-old imported sedan. The house is as formal on the inside as it is out front, if a little better preserved. Where the shutters are fading on the facade, the interior reads like a page from *Architectural Digest* circa 1992. Pale peach walls and pooled drapery abound.

Joey and I make our way through the sunken living room, not bothering to take off our shoes. French doors off a stiff, plastic-covered chintz family room lead to the upper terrace of the backyard. I pause with one hand on the door.

Mrs. Kim is kneeling in front of an explosion of David Austin roses like a nun at the altar. A giant hat that matches the floral living room drapes protects her pale perfect skin from the sun. For a moment, she looks like Maggie and I can almost pretend.

But then she rocks back on her heels and I see the expression on her face. Peaceful, in a way Maggie never was.

In a way that's out of place for a woman whose only daughter died yesterday.

"Mrs. Kim?"

She jumps, a gardening glove flung to her throat.

"Oh, you startled me," she says in her softly accented English. I think Mrs. Kim wanted to be an actress—she has the feel of a starlet playing at being a Korean-American housewife. Old-world gentility and Western wiles. At least I know where Maggie got the idea.

"Sorry to scare you," I say.

Joey clears his throat, shifts nervously behind me. "Hi, Mrs. Kim."

He seems to fade more than step back into the house. This is the boy who found their daughter's body. If the police had considered foul play, Joey would be the prime suspect. As it is, he acts guilty. He's the one who opened Schrödinger's box. If he hadn't come over, hadn't found the body, as far as any of us would know, Maggie'd still be alive.

To us, anyway. At least until the pool guy came.

Joey makes his excuses and exits, shutting the French doors behind him. Mrs. Kim and I regard each other blankly until the latch clicks shut, like a starting pistol. She immediately assumes the stoic expression of a woman suffering another loss in a long, painful life. You would almost believe she had weathered a war, lost people a lifetime ago. Maybe she had. She sighs and climbs to her feet.

I step toward her, close enough to see that the perfect skin is turning to crepe. Her lipstick bleeds just outside the edge of her sad smile, into the lines of age.

She pulls off her gloves and drops them to the slate patio. I reach out and take both her hands in my own. It's as close to a hug as Mrs. Kim and I have ever managed.

"I'm glad you're back," she says, her voice suddenly thick with emotion.

"I don't know what to say," I admit. "I . . ." Words skitter away and I squeeze Mrs. Kim's hands instead.

She seems to recall herself and pulls away, exclaiming

like a schoolgirl from another century, "Oh, goodness! My hands are so dirty. Let me wash them. Come inside. Violetta made iced tea this morning. I'm sure Parker hasn't finished it all."

I follow her back in through the dim cave of the house, thick white carpets and double-high ceilings fighting for the right to swallow every sound.

Joey is nowhere in sight. Through the windowpane set into the front door, I can see his escape route. He's waiting on the curb, leaning against his car. Crying.

"So, obviously, Maggie didn't have a will, but I'm sure she'd be happy for you to have anything that you want of hers," Mrs. Kim says, scrubbing her hands furiously at the kitchen sink.

I stand across from her at the large granite-topped island and lean in to smell a vase of red roses. Mrs. Kim only grows pinks and whites. Pulling back from the vase, I see the card from the florist, tucked into a small envelope. Sympathy flowers, then. Red. An odd choice. Unless they were from someone who knew Maggie well. Pink and white might suit Mrs. Kim, but her daughter's tastes ran darker. Flowers were just the start.

"You know where the glasses are," Mrs. Kim continues, pointing the way with her chin. I go to the cupboard and take down two tumblers, filling them from a half-empty pitcher of iced green tea off the door of the double-wide commercial-grade fridge.

"We're thinking Thursday for the funeral. Enough time for my brother and parents to fly out from Korea," Mrs. Kim says. "I'll let you know . . . send an e-mail or something, when the plans are finalized. If you wouldn't mind telling her friends. I don't know them all, but they are welcome to come." She dries her hands on a waffle-weave towel and takes a long drink of the tea I pass to her.

"I needed that. It's so hot today," she says conversationally, taking off her hat. She fans her face with the brim before dropping it to the counter, her eyes fixed on some point over my shoulder. "Oh, Jude." She says my name softly, like a curse word, like a prayer.

"I always knew Maggie would go to Hell," she says. "It's hard for a mother to know that about her own child." Her eyes drift to mine. "You understand?"

A spike of anger goes through me. But I nod, to keep her talking, to keep from saying anything I can't take back.

Mrs. Kim looks down at the water rings our glasses have left on the countertop. She picks up her hat, drops it, does it again. "It wasn't too late for redemption. But she's made sure of it now. You see, I knew about the nights she'd sneak out, or have her friends over. The boys, the smoking, the running around. A mother knows. But suici . . ." She can't say it and swallows the word. "My baby died, and I didn't even feel her go."

Finally, this eggshell of a woman cracks, sudden tears aging her face a thousand years. She grips the counter with both hands as if it's a dial that can reverse death. But the counter remains unmoved. A moment later, her crying jag done, she wipes her face with a napkin I pull from the rooster-shaped holder on the counter and dashes the tears from her eyes.

"I'm tired," she tells me. "I think I'll lie down. Go on out to the pool house. Take whatever you'd like. Violetta can see you out."

I nod and watch Mrs. Kim glide away into the foyer and up the curving stairs. She looks nothing like her daughter now. She looks defeated.

Even beaten and battered, Maggie never did. Then again, the only beatings Maggie took were by choice.

Once Mrs. Kim is gone, I text Joey to meet me out back. I'm ready now. I want him to tell me the rest of what he saw, how he found her. I don't stop to think that it might bother him to return to the scene of her death.

It's funny. I always thought I'd be the one to find

Maggie's body. I was the one on speed dial for every cri-
sis. But she didn't call me that night. Who did she call
instead? If not me and not Joey, then maybe no one. But
something just doesn't feel right.

———————————————————————

"I'm going to do it," she said. "It's the only way."

"What?" I was in my room, under the covers, cell
phone pressed to my ear. I could barely understand her
through her sobs.

"I'm better off dead," Maggie said. "I already know
a way. And then I'll be fine. Okay? I just wanted you to
know. I love you."

"Maggie, don't be stupid," I said, already out of bed,
stealing my mother's car keys, trying not to scream. If I
screamed, I'd wake the house, wasting time. "I'm coming."

"Don't." Maggie had stopped crying. She sounded
resigned.

I moved faster, starting the car, still in my pajamas.

"Maggie, wait."

"If only you knew," she said, and hung up.

I dropped the phone and ran a stop sign to reach her in
time. Raced through the side yard, clanging the gate loud
enough to set the neighbor's Pekingese yapping. I slipped,

skidding alongside the swimming pool, and landed at the front step of the pool house, a one-room stucco cottage at the back of the yard that had been her room since she was fifteen.

I slammed into the front door, throwing it open.

"Well, you took your time," Maggie said.

No blood on the floor, no bottle of pills, no pile of tissues or tear streaks or broken glass. Just Maggie on the sofa—a graying hand-me-down from the eighties—her cordless phone in one hand. "She's here, gotta go."

She hung up with whoever and grinned at me. "Want a G and T? I smuggled a bottle from the big house yesterday." She rose and rummaged through the mini fridge in the tiny kitchenette, emerging with a large bottle of Bombay Sapphire. Resting it on the coffee table with a heavy thunk, she dropped back onto the sofa, arranged her pink cat-print pajamas, and took a drag from one of those damned filterless cigarettes.

"Well?" she said, looking at me—shaking, queasy with fear and anger, collapsed against the front door.

"Well, what?" I managed to say. "I thought you'd be dead."

"I *am* dying. Of boredom. I call it a surprise slumber party. You like? Starts with a bang." She stubbed out her cigarette and stretched like a cat. "Oh, don't pout. Take off your coat and have a drink. We'll watch a movie. *That Touch of Mink* just ended." She pointed to the TV with her glass. Doris Day's credit was rolling by. "But another one's about to begin."

The pool house is empty now. The little building seems to sag, the stucco faded, the windows dark. No stench of burning cigarettes, no glasses of gin and tonic. The bed is unmade and there's a half-eaten bowl of popcorn on the counter. The thrift store décor is no longer ironic, just tattered and worn without the glamour girl for a foil.

I pace the room. She didn't leave a note. Then again, most suicides don't. I sit on the sofa, staring at the unmade bed on the opposite wall, the TV stand that swivels to face either one, depending on where she lay. The TV is facing me. I wonder if the dent in the mattress matches her hips.

Maggie, what did you do?

Joey knocks outside.

"Come in."

"You all right?" he asks. I should be the one asking him.

"Yeah," I say. "Just thinking."

"About what?"

"Pajama parties." I brush my hair from my face. "Her mom said I could take anything I wanted."

"Yeah," Joey says. "She told me that too."

I look up at him. "What did you take?"

Joey blushes and I'm afraid he's going to say underwear or something equally perverted. Instead he points to the low bookshelf at the foot of the bed, the one holding up the TV on its swivel stand.

"I lent her my copy of *Cyrano de Bergerac* in ninth grade. I just took it back."

I nod, relieved. Maggie has a lot of things that are mine. Things that come with being the same dress size and in the same classes—borrowed clothes, forgotten books. But I don't want them back. She should go into the afterlife with some possessions.

All I really want are answers.

I move over to the bed and lie down on it. Joey watches me self-consciously. The dent in the mattress is too big for my hips. I sit up suddenly. Maggie wasn't alone here last night. I jump up from the bed, wondering if the cops bothered to check it for blood, hair, or other things. I go into the top drawer of her tiny dresser, pulling out her underwear and lingerie.

"Oh, Christ," Joey says, his mind going to where mine had been a few minutes before.

"Shut up. I'm looking for her pink slip." She'd bought it as a joke in the old-lady section of Macy's where they still sold the girdles and undergarments our grandmothers wore. A pale pink slip with tea-colored lace around the edges. She said it made her feel glamorous, like an old-time Hollywood movie star. It was her favorite outfit for seducing new boys. It made her confident, and the thin fabric outlined her "assets."

"It's not here." I check the hamper. Empty. "You said you found her in the pool?"

Joey clears his throat, sounding oddly strangled when he speaks. "Yes."

"In a swimsuit?" I ask.

"Um, no. In a nightgown or something. I thought she was naked at first. It clung to her."

I hang my head. "Pink. With tan lace."

Joey nods. "And a tiny pink rose. Right here." He presses his finger to the middle of his chest. "I kept staring at it when I did CPR, thinking if the rose rises, she's breathing, she's alive."

"Huh," I say. It comes out as a sob.

"What? Does that mean something?" he asks.

I nod, trying to force back my tears. "Yeah. It means she was sleeping with someone new." I rub my eyes. "What kind of drugs?"

Joey blinks. "What?"

"What. Kind. Of. Drugs. The coroner?"

Joey shakes his head. "I don't know. The EMTs mentioned it. Mr. Kim says they'll know in a few days."

I sit up and look at him. "What if somebody drugged her?"

His eyes flick across the unmade bed. "Like date rape?"

"Maybe. She didn't do pills."

Joey shrugs. "Well, even if someone had drugged her for sex, why toss her in the pool?"

I fish around in my bag for sunglasses and put them back on. "Chlorine? Maybe it washes away the evidence. They should at least look into it."

Joey is silent for a moment. "Yeah," he finally says. "I guess we'll know when the results come in." But I can see he's thinking now, no longer trying to avoid what I already know.

Maggie didn't kill herself. She was murdered.

3

We drive south, crossing streets with names like Alessandro, Bellefontaine, and Orange Grove. A hundred fifty years ago this place was a rancher's paradise. But the natives and Spaniards made way for orange groves and new Americans, like high school seniors making way for the next graduating class. To this day, the streets are named after the wealthiest families and the crops that made them rich. Never after the people who planted them.

The houses shift from double-lot mansions and Victorians, stately Italianate facades, and Craftsman houses with their dark woods and deep green plaster, to apartments and bungalows the size of Maggie's pool house.

If the Kims live in the big house, Joey and I live in the servants' quarters.

"Your mom home?" Joey asks when he drops me off in front of my place, a cracked stucco two-bedroom rental at the back of a three-house lot. Mrs. Feldenkrais is taking out her recycling. She looks a sight in her yellow house-dress, hair like spun cotton candy. Neither of us wave.

"Probably. We talked before my flight. She wanted to pick me up but I told her I needed to see you first."

"Well." Joey climbs out of the car and pulls my duffel out of the back. "If you want to get dinner later, call me. A few of us were going to . . . you know. Like a wake."

"A wake," I repeat, letting it sink in. I already know who will be there, Maggie's inner circle. Could one of them know the new bedfellow? "I'm in."

"Great." He hesitates, like he wants to say something else. His eyes flick to the house and back to me. He drums the heel of his hand on the car door. "Great. I'll pick you up at seven."

He leaves me standing on the curb, heels digging into the dead grass, pondering what just went unsaid. Heat rises from the pavement in waves. Seven hours ago, I was in a woodland paradise. I could be swimming in Danielle's Olympic-sized pool. I pick up my bag and walk to the house.

The front door is open, which means the AC is on

the blink again. The TV drones away in the living room. Someone sits on the old brown sofa. A man's hand raises a can of beer.

Roy. My mother's favorite mistake.

I go around to the backyard before he can see me, stumbling across the broken brick pathway to the rear door. I drop my bags on one side of the cement steps and sit down. A lemon tree wilts in the center of the yard, casting a thin shadow on a broken lawn chair.

I could call Joey again. He'd come get me. But then we'd have to talk about more than just Maggie. I'd rather face what's inside the house.

I peer into the dim crawl space behind the steps, shove my duffel bag inside, and stand up, shouldering my backpack. I'll go to the movies or the library. My mother will be home eventually. Or it'll be time to go to Maggie's wake.

My eyes drift closed for a second, long enough for me to realize I'm too tired to keep going. I give up the dodge game and unlock the back door. I enter through the kitchen, my recovered suitcase trailing crumbs of yellow dust from beneath the house. The TV still plays in the living room. I hear him cough.

My stomach buckles. Roy and I don't mix. Not if I can help it.

I turn into the hallway and slip into my room, locking the door before I collapse, face-first, onto my bed.

"I slept with him, you know." Sophomore year. Maggie and I were dipping our toes into her then-boyfriend Keith's pool.

We'd seen each other around freshman year. I was the new kid in town, she was the one who fit in, even with the seniors. But it wasn't until that spring that she took notice and invited me into her world. A world with pools like Keith's, overlandscaped monstrosities with fake boulders and a fire pit in the Jacuzzi. Maggie said it looked like a watering hole from *The Lion King*.

In the house, Keith and Joey were playing video games with Keith's older brother, Scott, online. Scott was stationed somewhere overseas where they still had Nintendo and Internet access twenty-four hours a day.

"Who?" I asked. I felt like a child next to Maggie in her black one-piece, her butterfly kimono flared out behind her like wings. My toenails were unpainted. I wore no makeup. I was fifteen and looked like I was twelve. Maggie was my age, going on twenty-five.

"Scott. Corporal Punishment over there." She pointed

with her chin, meaning the house where the boys were online, or maybe the country where Scott was stationed.

"You slept with your boyfriend's older brother," I said, deadpan.

Maggie laughed. "Don't be disgusting. Keith wasn't my boyfriend then. We were just hanging out and there was Scott with those puppy-dog eyes, all 'I'm going to war and may never come back.' It was, I don't know, exciting. The whole life-and-death thing. What if I was his last chance to get laid by an American chick? So I did it."

I took it all in without comment, resting my chin on my knees. When she didn't say any more, I asked, "How was it?"

Maggie sighed and stretched out on her towel. "Oh, you know how boys are. There's the sensitive ones that get all weepy and 'I love you' if you let them touch you, and the douche bags that go all cold and stoic once they get their rocks off. I was kind of hoping for a douche bag. I mean, soldiers are macho, right? But nope, he was the other kind."

I looked at her, expecting a joke. "You'd rather have a jerk than a guy that loves you?"

Maggie sat up on an elbow and turned her heart-shaped sunglasses my way. "Honey, if a boy only says he loves you after you've screwed him, it ain't you he loves, it's your Bermuda Triangle. Much more honest to have a wham-bam-thank-you-ma'am than a post-party love fest. Even better if they're a little rough, so there's no confusion."

"Rough," I repeated, swallowing my disgust.

"Yeah, why not?" Maggie smiled a little. "I've gotten a shiner or two in my day. It's primal. You know, exciting."

"Like screwing your boyfriend's brother because he might die in the war?"

Maggie pouted. "Don't get all high and mighty on me. Have you seen my parents? I can't believe they ever did it enough to have me and Parker. It's like they're stone. I'd rather smack and get smacked every once in a while. At least I'd be feeling something."

"What's wrong with just love?" I asked.

Maggie snorted. "God, you sound like a virgin. Seriously." She shook her head.

I tucked my knees back beneath my chin. Maggie looked at me over the rims of her starlet sunglasses. "Seriously?" she repeated. "You're a virgin?"

I shrugged, embarrassed, but I didn't answer. She laughed, which hurt, but then she clapped me on the shoulder, which didn't. "What's that like?" she asked, as if she'd never been a virgin, a born Venus, unable to relate.

I pulled my legs closer and sniffed at her.

She laughed again and hugged me. "Don't let the bastards touch you," she said. "You're too good for them."

It was my turn to laugh, a tightly held little snort. I wanted to hug her back.

I slap my hand against the wall and come awake, sweating. My phone is ringing, buzzing from my backpack. Someone is knocking on my door.

"Honey? Are you in there?"

I ignore the door and grab the phone. It goes to voice mail as I slide it open.

A text appears. Joey is parked outside. "Shit." I comb my hair out of my face and wipe my sweat onto my pillow.

It's not dark yet, but a breeze has picked up. I feel it filtering through my window. My room is small at the best of times, enough space for a twin bed, a closet, and a dresser that doubles as a desk. In summertime, the bed is like a coffin and the window seems to shrink down to a pinhole, for all the air it lets in.

I get up, change into jeans and a new top. I grab a hoodie and open the door.

"Hi, Mom," I say. "Gotta run."

She blinks at me with the same eyes I see in the mirror every day. Daddy might be long gone, but there's no hiding who my mother is.

"Oh. So soon?" she asks. "I thought Roy and I could take you to dinner." She reaches a hand out to touch my shoulder. "You know, talk." Her voice is soft with velvet empathy. God, how I hate that tone.

"Can't," I say. "Joey's here. We're having a wake."

"A wake? Oh . . . well, then we'll go with you. You know I loved Maggie like a daughter."

I smile. As her real daughter, I know exactly what that's worth. Way too little, far too late.

"Honey, that face looks ghastly. But you're grieving." My mother criticizes and reverses with economic speed. "Come on, I'll take you and maybe Roy can join us."

Her hand is on my shoulder like a small, persistent hug. I shake my head. "Joey's already here. Kids only."

My mother sighs like she's just finished the dishes and I'm piling more into the sink. She lets go of my shoulder. "All right, then. Do you need money?"

Before I can answer, she's dug into her purse and is peeling off bills. She shoves two twenties at me, then adds another, the way some parents might add a kiss on the forehead—firmly pressed and dry against the skin. I flee through the front door, barely registering the empty sofa or the fallen can drained of beer.

"Let's go," I say, but Joey's a good getaway man. He's already starting the car. I pull the door closed behind me.

His eyes flick off the road for a second. "Everything all right?" I shrug and burrow into my seat. Joey looks at me. "Jude?"

"What?"

He turns his attention back toward the road. Here it comes, the unsaid question. The chance to explain myself. If only I could. But Joey skips the heart of the problem and goes for the jugular instead.

"Maggie said your mom's boyfriend is a dick. That's why you and I . . . why we . . . That's why you went back east this summer." He stumbles over the politics of us. The same line we'd been stumbling over since the spring. "If he's still being a dick, I want to know."

My stomach takes a dive. I laugh and shake my head. Seven lousy weeks and Maggie couldn't keep her mouth shut. I want to tell Joey to fuck off. Ask about us, sure, about what went wrong. But this Roy crap is none of his business. If Maggie meant to protect me, she should've stuck around, not blabbed about it.

How much did she tell him? Enough for him to worry

about me. But is it also enough for him to understand me too?

I let go of the breath I've been holding. Poor Joey. I'm angry at Maggie, but she's gone, and he's right here. Hurting him won't punish her.

"It's fine," I say, and I hear my voice crack. I clear my throat and buckle my seat belt. It *is* fine, truth be told. I lock my door when I'm here, and stay away when I can. Given my mom's track record with men, I'll outlast Roy no problem. No problem at all.

"Just drive, please." My voice is solid again.

Joey drives, but he's got one eye on me, taking it all in. I feel naked and I don't like it, so I put on my sunglasses and crank his iPod up as loud as it will go.

4

The restaurant of choice is a small Mediterranean place in one of those squat brick storefronts on Colorado Boulevard. Swathed in pricey chain boutiques and chock-full of tourists from LA proper.

Joey parks with the valet. I stand there, shivering from the chill of a sudden easterly wind. The tops of the San Gabriel Mountains are growing angry with clouds. It'll pass. Just like the rest of it.

We go inside. Dane and Tallulah are sitting in a back room at a round table for eight. Tallulah waves us over. She and Dane are the closest things to parents in the motley family of friends gathering tonight. They've been dating since freshman year. I'd vote them most likely to be married before college. After that, maybe most likely to split. Higher education isn't for the faint of heart or for those who fall in love too young.

Still, they're stable right now, when it counts. Tally probably made the reservation for this thing. She's the sort to even call in and up the count by one to fit me.

Half the seats are still empty. No-shows? I wonder. Or kids who think dinner parties and wakes are the sort of things you cruise by on the way to better plans? It's still summer after all. The dead can wait forever.

"You're here," Tallulah says, holding her hands out to me. Her charm bracelets slide down her thin wrists with a cymbal-like clash, bruising the tops of my fingers. She squeezes tight and pulls me in for a double-cheeked kiss and another meaningful squeeze. Tallulah's got pale, perfect skin and brown eyes like hot-fudge sundaes—warm and sweet, with an ice-cold center. She hugs Joey and steers us toward two empty seats.

Tallulah is funeral-ready. She's already wearing black— all black hose and a matching miniskirt peering out from the hem of a man's pin-striped blazer, sleeves artfully rolled up to give her bracelets free rein. Dane wears black jeans and a black button-down shirt. All business, but he still looks casual. I feel underdressed. But then the rest of the group trickles in and we're all just as patched together as ever.

Hank and Eppie arrive in what can only be described as hippie surfer chic—woven Guatemalan pullovers with kangaroo pouches across the front, cutoff jeans, and flip-flops. Hank's got highlights in his blond shag. Eppie's hair is buzzed a short, spiky black. Her peeling manicure matches in length and color. She plops down next to me, smelling of limes, salt, and beer.

"Hey, sweets," she says, and gives me a hair ruffle of sympathy. And then Edina Rodriguez wafts in like a whiff of cheap perfume.

Edina was Maggie's other best friend. Maggie used to joke that she'd never seen the two of us in the same room together because we were the same person. Truth is, we can't stand each other. Maggie loved me, told me her secrets. Edina wanted in but never got it.

She shoots daggers at me from across the table and I see her eyes are red—from pot or crying. When she sees me looking, she smiles and tosses her dark brown hair. She's wearing a short choker strand of pearls, and she makes sure I see them. Those were Maggie's pearls, part of her polished-debutante collection—Maggie dressed like a Barbie doll, never in clothes, always in costumes.

What Edina is doing with them on her thick little neck, I couldn't guess, but if Maggie shared her pearls, she might have also shared something else. Like the name of the boy in her bed.

I stare Edina down and she blinks first. She looks away, clutching at the necklace, and begins to cry in silent, shuddering tears. I let her. Dane offers her his napkin and leans over to kiss her forehead. Lucky for me, contestant number eight has arrived.

Luke Liu, aka Lukey Loo, pulls up the last chair. Luke is one of those not-quite-first-generation Chinese kids who pointedly avoids all things Chinese, including other people. The fact that he ran in a circle with any other Asians at all would be a mystery if the Asian in question hadn't been Maggie.

Luke has been in love with Maggie since the first grade, when he came to the States and still spoke mostly Chinese. Maggie didn't speak Mandarin, of course, but she apparently spoke "little boy" back then just as well as she spoke "grown man" later. He was wrapped around her finger in an instant. Luke lost his accent for Maggie. And gained his nickname from ogling her as they grew up.

The kid had foresight. Maggie was worth ogling, as it turned out. I couldn't help but wonder if, the night she died, Lukey Loo was watching her too.

"Pictures. Full-sized freaking photographs," Maggie said over the phone one night. I was sprawled on my bed writing a term paper on Virginia Woolf. She was in her pool house sipping champagne and burning cigarettes.

"Like black-and-white?" I asked. "Surveillance should always be in grainy black-and-white."

"Black-and-white, full-color, freaking infrared—you name it. He'd give me the creeps if he wasn't so harmless. I think of him as rape prevention. If anything ever goes wrong on a date, Luke's got his eye out for me."

I could hear her flipping through the portfolio of photographs Luke had accidentally left behind in the band room. He'd been mooning over it all day, so naturally Maggie had gotten curious. And light-fingered.

"Jesus," she said. "He's my psychotic little guardian angel." She inhaled and sighed. "Doesn't make me look half bad either."

Lukey Loo smiles at me from across the table. Fate or irony has placed him next to Edina. I nod and he drops the smile, as if only just remembering someone has died. Then I see why. Joey has dragged another chair over and is trying to wedge it in between his seat and Tallulah's.

I scooch over to make way for it.

A disinterested busboy dresses the table with an extra setting. Joey nods at him and places the knife and fork in an X over the empty plate. He returns to his own chair, warming the space beside me. The new seat stays empty and cold as the void.

"Way to sober up a room, Joey," Dane says resentfully. I give Dane a once-over while the busboy returns with ice water all around.

Joey raises his glass, cubes already melting. "To Maggie."

The glasses rise and fall like a broken concertina. Tallulah's comes up last, regret clear on her face that the toast hadn't been her idea. Joey tips his glass against Maggie's empty one. He's just shown more class than any of us.

Under the table, I scratch his leg affectionately. He nods and grabs my hand in a brief grip.

We sit, the eight of us, swaddled in the moment, each grieving in our own way. And I can feel it, that sinking undertow, like being swallowed whole.

So I shatter the mood.

"Anybody know who Maggie fucked the night she died?"

Edina inhales her water and coughs it out explosively. Hank and Eppie burst out laughing. Luke has turned pale and is looking anywhere but at me. Dane has another sip of water, cool as a breeze. Tallulah bangs the table with her fist, her charm bracelets making a racket that turns heads at other tables.

"That—" she says. And the waiter arrives.

"Do you need more time?" he asks in that chirpy superior/subservient tone only actors can perfect. I smile up at him. We all need more time, especially Maggie. "Just a touch," I say.

"I could order," Hank offers.

"Lamb shank," Joey says.

You don't have to try hard to imagine what dinners are like at Hank's or Joey's house. Don't let a little drama hold you up—a boy's got to eat.

The rest of the table places their orders either in embarrassed mumbles or deep, meditational sighs.

"Just water," I say. I'm hungrier for an answer than anything on the menu just yet.

The waiter scowls at me—can't expect a tip on a glass of water—and leaves. My leg is shaking under the table, pumping an invisible gas pedal, driving me on. One of these sycophants might know who killed Maggie.

I survey the table and smile. "Well?"

Silence and the clink of distant forks reply.

"Did I embarrass someone? Was it one of you? I won't tell. Just . . ." I wave my hand in the air. "Close your eyes and raise your thumbs." Like a game of Seven Up. No one would need to know but me. And maybe the cops.

"Jesus, you are one crazy jealous bitch," Tally says. I raise an eyebrow and direct my gaze toward Dane.

"Takes one . . . ," I counter. She exhales in frustration.

"Dudes," Eppie says. "We're all hurting here. Can't we just, you know, toast our friend and let it be?"

"Sure, Eppie." I nod. "My bad. Everyone"—I raise my water glass in salute—"pretend I'm drunk. Now, carry on."

I slouch back into my seat and everyone does carry on for a moment or two. The edge of tension is blunted. I shrug back into my hoodie and lower my eyelids to half-mast. Maybe I should apologize. This wake is for Maggie, after all. We're all here for Maggie.

I start to speak.

"She had just told me she'd gotten into Brown," Edina says suddenly. My breath hitches and I raise an eyebrow. Everyone knew Maggie wanted to go to Brown more than anything. But I thought I was the only one who knew she'd applied early. I guess Maggie didn't tell me all her secrets. Clearly, she'd been spreading them around.

"Really?" Eppie says. "Awesome surf in Rhode Island. I would have visited her."

"Yeah." Edina beams, sounding pleased to have had the scoop on something for once. She looks to me for corroboration. I give her a Mona Lisa smile and turn my head before looking away.

My napkin twists in my hands. Maggie's dreams had been just over the horizon. Whoever took them from her is going to pay.

"Anyone know when the funeral is?" Luke asks. I imagine he'll want to have his cameras all cleaned and ready by then.

"Thursday," Joey says.

"Do you guys remember when Maggie said she was too pretty to be buried and wanted a glass coffin like Snow White?" Luke continues. "Do you think they'll do that?"

"She killed herself," Tally snaps. "You don't have open caskets for suicides."

I glare laser beams. "It wasn't suicide."

Tally all but sticks her tongue out at me, daring me to make another scene.

"Either way, she drowned facedown in a swimming pool," Hank says. Joey and I don't bother to correct him. He shakes his head. "Closed casket for sure."

"Oh," Luke says, and falls silent again, his dream photo op gone.

"How's Parker taking it? I'd hate to be him right now," Hank says.

"No kidding," Luke adds. "Like it's not hard enough being the only son." Luke's in the same boat as Parker, with one sister in tow. Only, in Luke's case, he's also the oldest, which must come with some privileges. Like more free time for stalking.

"Parker's holding up," Joey says noncommittally.

I haven't seen him myself, but knowing how the Kims baby him, Parker's probably right as rain.

"Why did you say that?" Edina asks me. I debate ignoring her, but she asks again. "Why don't you think it was a suicide?"

"Because I know Maggie," I say slowly, to make myself clear. "She wouldn't do that."

Edina frowns. "And you think she had sex with somebody? Why? Did the cops find something?"

I shrug. I haven't spoken to the cops. They might have found a yeti for all I know.

I sit up. "Call it intuition." And an unmade bed. "Hey, you were best buds, right, Eddie?" I say, using Maggie's nickname for her. My eyes fall on the pearl necklace—a gift Maggie would have never bestowed willingly. "Don't you know?"

Edina unconsciously fingers her pearls, no point to make this time. She looks pained. So I guess she didn't know either. She glances up and her eyes confirm it.

Joey puts a warning hand on my leg, like a dad trying to keep a little kid from running into the street.

The waiter shows up just then with a busboy and a tray full of dinner. While the rest of them stare at their food, I sigh and look around the room again.

Tallulah is sulking with her wrists folded across her chest, bracelets forming a protective shield. Dane idly plays with her hair, sipping on his water like it's scotch. He smacks his lips and gives me a wolf's smile. I give him the finger. He smiles even wider.

Maggie always laughed at Dane's signature bad-boy look. But I've never been one for male entitlement, so I take a different approach.

"Hey, Dane, how's the gonorrhea?"

He frowns and looks away.

Tallulah pulls back from him. "You son of a bitch. You told?"

I try not to laugh, but a smile makes it to the surface anyway. Rumors make good arrows. Sometimes they strike true.

"Have you heard?" Maggie leaned into me, breathless with news.

It was after school in March, the beginning of the end of our junior year. I was sitting on the hill overlooking the campus parking lot, watching the kids lucky enough to have cars head home. I was carless and carefree in the midst of a homework picnic, textbooks and notebooks arrayed around me, when Maggie appeared and plopped down, crushing my geometry homework.

"Hey!" I rescued the crumpled pages from beneath her knees. "Paper doesn't grow on trees."

Maggie made a face. "Hardee har har. Are you even listening to me?"

I smoothed out the pages and sighed. "Now I am. You have my full attention."

She situated herself, folding her legs into a half lotus yoga position. The privilege of someone with dance training and a fitness coach. "Dane is screwing some freshman from Rosemead."

"What?" I closed my textbook, attention officially snagged. "Dane's cheating on Tally? Does she know?" The implication made my fingers tingle and my eyes go wide. Dane and Tallulah had been an item since we were freshmen. Three years was an eternity. Everyone expected them to go all the way, as in graduation, college, a ring, babies. "Wait. How do you know?"

Maggie grinned like the Cheshire cat. "Yes, no, the school nurse."

"What does that mean?"

"Yes, he's cheating. No, Tally doesn't know yet, and I overheard the school nurse talking to Mrs. Vogt in the front office. It seems this girl passed on a little 'rash' or something." She made air quotes around the word "rash." "Dane thought it was jock itch." Maggie broke into peals of laughter. "The nurse told him he had to notify his girlfriend, that it could cause problems. I guess he thought he had doctor-patient confidentiality or something because, when the nurse offered to tell Tallulah, he confessed it wasn't her. The nurse was in the office calling the girl's school to reach her. Isn't that awful? Truly awful for her and for Tally, but Dane's such a douche. He had it coming."

"STDs are no joke," I said, finding it hard to join the laughter.

"Says the virgin." Maggie slapped my arm. "Come on. Enjoy this. You don't even like Dane."

"He's Tallulah's boyfriend. I don't like either of them."

Maggie shrugged. "Tally's not so bad. And at least she keeps Dane from macking on the rest of us."

"Yeah, except now he's poaching at Rosemead."

Maggie laughed and lay back, resting her head on a stack of my textbooks. I lay down next to her.

"We should tell Tallulah," I said.

"Nope." Maggie folded her hands behind her head. "*He* should tell her. I told him so."

I sat up on an elbow to read her face. "You *told* him? He knows you know?"

Maggie shrugged. "Somebody's got to keep him honest. Besides, isn't that what friends are for?"

Dane is pleading with Tally in the corner. Maybe I went too far. I push back from the table. "I've got to powder my nose."

Eppie smirks. Joey sighs and drops his hand off my leg.

I take my time in the ladies' room, reading the adverts on the inside of the stall door. Teeth whitening and a limo service. It's like a how-to for desperate people—fake smile and rented opulence for only $299. I'm suddenly tired, like the autoflush is pulling me down. I'd say it's jet lag, the adrenaline of the past hour draining way. But it's worse than that. I stand up. Just a little more face time lies between me and a good night's sleep. Everything will look brighter in the morning. My mom used to say that.

I'm splashing water on my face in preparation for round two at the table when the door opens with the alacrity of a ringing bell. It's Edina. She pushes it shut behind her, leaning against it to keep anyone else out, and me in.

"Edina," I say with a nod of acknowledgment. I squee-gee my face over the sink with one hand, waving the other in front of the automatic paper towel dispenser. I tear the towel free and bury my face in it. When I come up for air, Edina's still there, watching me.

"I'm sorry," I say. "I'll get out of your way." I move toward the door.

"That would be a first," she scoffs. But she doesn't move. Her arms are folded across her chest. "I don't get it. What did Maggie ever see in you?"

I take in Edina, her eyes tiny in her angry face. There's a catch in her black nylons that's threatening to run. Her nails are painted, and bitten to the quick.

I smile and blow my nose on the wadded toweling in my hand. "I was just about to ask you the same thing."

She scowls at me. "I'm serious, Jude. You're obnoxious, rude, surly. You rub everybody the wrong way."

"Not true," I say, tossing the towel and resting my back against the sink. "Just you, Tallulah and Dane. Everybody else loves me."

"Why?" she asks again, ignoring my quip. The look on her face is intense, bordering on desperate.

"Because Tallulah's fake perfect and Dane's an ass, and I don't let them forget it. And you? You, I just don't like. No offense."

Edina laughs, a little hiccupping noise. "Oh, now why would I be offended?"

I shrug. "Some people might be."

"Maggie liked me," Edina says, like it's supposed to hurt me. Like friendships are monogamous. But clearly, if the tableful of people outside are any indication, there was plenty of Maggie to go around. "That should be enough for you."

I raise an eyebrow. "Enough for me to what?"

"To accept me. To let me be a part of the group."

It's my turn to laugh. "Clearly, you *are* part of the group. You're here, aren't you? Hell, even Maggie didn't make the cut tonight. Just you, me, and the Little Rascals out there."

"How can you be so flip about it?" Edina snaps. "Maggie's dead." She's starting to tear up.

I clench my jaw, refusing to go down that rabbit hole with her. "I know, Eddie. And here you are, cornering me in the bathroom, asking me to play nice. Isn't that just a bit off point?"

"You just called me Eddie. Maggie called me that."

"I know. I was there."

"What else do you know about me? I mean, did she ever talk about me?"

I sigh. "If she did, Edina, I swear I wasn't listening. Look. You're upset. I get it. You loved Maggie, so did I. Don't you want to know why she died?"

"No!" Her face crumples and she's crying now, full bore, nose running and everything. I wave another paper towel from the dispenser and hand it to her.

"I don't want to know what would make someone so . . . so . . . so much better than us kill herself. I mean, if life is too hard for Maggie Kim, then how are the rest of us supposed to . . ." She trails off and I see the shadows around her eyes are from more than just smudged Maybelline.

At this point in the script, I'm supposed to give Edina a hug and seal the rift between us. Or fall into it together, one big crying jag that makes us besties for life. But this isn't a movie. "Take your time. Pull yourself together."

She blows her nose and stands there snuffling.

"Maybe you should talk to someone," I suggest.

Edina blinks at me in disbelief. "I thought I was."

I glance past her, unwilling to see the bruised look in her eyes again. I've got enough bruises of my own. "I meant, like, a friend."

Edina surprises me by laughing. She throws her head back and rolls her eyes heavenward. "God, you are such a bitch."

She snatches another paper towel and uses it to open the bathroom door. "You know," she says, "Maggie had this picture. A happy little girl in a sundress. She showed it to me once, told me it was you when you were nine. She said it was proof you were a good person. Like no one could smile like that and not be."

My jaw clenches again, unexpectedly. Edina scans my face like it's a bar code, trying to get my number. I don't give it to her.

She shakes her head with a soft snort. "Must've come with the frame."

I manage a quirked smile. "Must have."

The door swings shut behind her and I collapse against the sink.

That version of me, the little girl with the celluloid smile? That was another thing I shared with Maggie. And only her. A butterfly in my stomach flaps its ugly wings. I feel betrayed.

I wash my hands, stalling for time. It's either that, or punch someone.

The door opens again and Eppie enters, grinning. If I stay in here any longer, I wonder if Tallulah will come in and join the fun, too.

"It's like a revolving door in here. What's going on?" I ask.

Eppie shakes her head. "Girl, what did you do to Edina?"

I shrug. "Nothing she didn't do right back to me."

Eppie snorts and hands me a paper towel. "And so comes the end of another fine meal."

"Is it over already?"

Eppie leans against the row of sinks and pulls out a cigarette from her bag. I can smell the bright scent of cloves as she puts it to her lips, unlit. "Already? That was the longest meal of my life." She groans and shakes her whole body like a dog drying itself off. She looks in the mirror and frowns at the cigarette before putting it back in the pack.

"Besides, who can eat at a time like this?" She shakes her head and exhales. "This was way too 'grown-up' for my taste." She picks a piece of tobacco off her tongue. "Hank and I were thinking of something a bit more relaxed Tuesday night, on the beach at Dockweiler, or up at Blue House."

Blue House is Eppie's dad's place in Eagle Rock. She splits her time between her mom's town house in Pasadena and the weathered blue Craftsman her dad, Mike, rents across the freeway overlooking Downtown LA. Mike is an old hippie, tanned as a piece of leather and mellow from a lifetime of weed. His girlfriend, Shasta, reads tarot cards for everyone at their house parties. Maggie was more of a champagne-and-caviar girl, but even she could not deny the bohemian tug of Blue House.

"God bless you, Eppie child." I kiss her on top of her spiky hair, breathing in the faint scent of patchouli.

"Aw, Jude, you just need to hang in there, all right? Blue House. Tuesday. And then . . ." She spreads her hands like seaweed on the water and I fill in the blanks.

Then we bury Maggie, then we make it through the summer and the rest of our lives. In another few weeks, we move on to our senior year, the beginnings of our last good-byes.

Maggie's death is a training ground for all the other endings we'll face this year. She's the wake-up call that says you're not a kid anymore. Tally knew it with her buttoned-up, adult dinner party. Clearly, I did not.

The ladies' room suddenly feels too small to hold us both.

"You got a ride home?" Eppie asks.

"Joey's got me."

"I bet he does." She winks and slips sideways so we can open the door to the world outside.

"Not very subtle," Joey says as we climb back into his car.

We're the last to leave. The valet, a young guy with a name tag that says "Chico," closes the door for me. I nod at him and shrug at Joey. "What can I say? I'm not Maggie."

Joey shakes his head in a way that says *fair enough.* "Where to now?" he asks.

I've done enough damage for one night, I decide. "Take me home."

Again, to his credit, Joey says nothing. He's a smart one. A classy guy. He pulls into the road and half smiles at me, the wind ruffling his hair.

It makes me wish life was normal again, that things could be different between us. But normal's been in my rearview mirror for a long time, and with Maggie gone, it's faded completely from view. Joey and I are friends. Good ones. And that's all we'll ever be.

5

The air smells like an East Coast autumn, like burning leaves. Joey points north toward the San Gabriel Mountains. A line of fire is marching across the foothills. In the moonlight, it looks like the dull red glow of a giant cigarette butt, bright on the front line, then cooling to a cinder. The wind gusts and for one moment, the fire burns brighter. Then we're surrounded by swirling ash, carried on the wind like an unfamiliar snow.

The house is quiet when he drops me off—my mom and Roy must be out. It's the first good news I've had in days.

Joey drives off and leaves me to unpack. I wash a load of laundry in the rickety machine at the back of the house and start the dryer before climbing into bed. Jet lag and grief make for good soporifics. To the click and roll of the dryer, I fall fast asleep.

I sit up in the middle of the night, wondering what woke me. The room is quiet. The air conditioner groans, shifting gears for another cooling cycle. I stretch out, cracking vertebrae up and down my spine.

The doorknob moves. It twists slowly, like someone is absentmindedly entering the room. I freeze. Despite the AC, I start to sweat.

But the door is locked. It stays closed.

"Welcome home, butterfly," a voice croons through the door.

Good night, Roy. Rest in Hell.

When I wake up again, it's still dark out, and the fires have gotten worse. My windowsill is lined with ash, and the air is dry enough to make my lips crack.

Last night, I dreamt Maggie, not Roy, was in Hell. Thanks to what Mrs. Kim said. That was one for the Hallmark aisle.

I look out the window. It's too early for the sun to be up, but my cell phone is buzzing. I check the text. It's

Eppie. She and Hank are headed to Malibu in that old beater pickup of theirs, with the Six-Pac camper shell on the back. Their own traveling beach cabana. *Surf's up*, the text says. *There's room for one more.*

Malibu, California. It's a thousand miles away from Pasadena as the car crawls, but only forty-five or so by map. Another Spanish rancho taken from the local natives, Malibu made its living from pottery and movies, not orange groves. Now the potteries are long gone, but the movie stars remain, and so do the wannabes. Traffic jams are epic along the Pacific Coast Highway in warm weather, even on a Monday. No wonder Eppie and Hank practically camp out there all summer long—they could save the planet with the gas they don't use driving back and forth.

The truck rattles to a stop. I wake up in the back, nestled in a pile of old blankets and towels.

This little hut is what makes a Six-Pac a Six-Pac—a gypsy caravan on the back of a pickup truck. During the summer, Hank and Eppie eat, sleep, and screw here. I'd never been inside before today.

In the dim light from the louvered panels along the door, I can just make out my surroundings—walls hung with bodhi seed beads and plastered with pictures of everything from giant, curling waves and fair-haired surf champs to the friendly face of the Indian elephant-headed god, Ganesh.

A dull ache throbs behind my eyes, in my chest. Time to make it through another day. I press a wrist to my head for support and breathe. Willing the ache to go away.

Maggie. Maggie. Maggie.

A gust of wind swirls around the cabin as Hank throws open the door, stirring the heady scent of patchouli oil, Nag Champa incense, and sweat.

"Morning, sunshine!" Hank says perkily. Like he's a cartoon alley cat on a fence, I throw my shoe at him.

"Grumpy!" he says, dodging it. He pulls two wet suits down from hooks on the wall. "Don't get up. We'll change out here. There's a suit somewhere beneath you when you're ready."

"Thanks," I growl, and nestle deeper into the old blanket wrapped around my shoulders. Morning and I aren't friends, but I'm glad Eppie texted me. Joey has a family thing and couldn't play chauffeur this morning. Besides which, he's still miffed at me for the way I acted at dinner last night. But that can't be helped. I'll make amends eventually. At least, that's what I tell myself. But I don't need to apologize to Hank or Eppie. They're too laid-back to be offended. I wipe the sleep from my eyes and drag myself into the daylight.

Eppie and Hank have been together for almost two years now. Maggie used to joke that when they finally got married, they would just tie themselves to each other with surfboard tethers instead of wedding rings.

Seeing them out on the waves together, it's not hard to believe.

It's an hour after dawn, disgustingly early in my book, but here we are at Point Dume. I sit on the back bumper of the truck, pulling the neoprene spring suit on over my tankini. Behind me, the bluffs rise in wrinkled sheets of stone and scrub. Out on the water, the wonder twins glide in the newly risen sunshine. The little cabin rots around me, salt air slowly eating away at the rusting brown-and-tan exterior. Six-Pacs, as a general rule, should have been shot in the head and put down long ago. But here in sunny SoCal, they live on. Like that farm parents tell their kids all the dead dogs go to. It's real, and it's called Malibu.

I can hear Eppie's shout of victory as she rides the next wave in. I walk down to the edge of the damp sand to meet her.

"Hey, Sleeping Beauty. Ready to greet the day?" Eppie's in a spring suit, tie-dyed purple neoprene that cuts off at her thighs and shoulders. She looks like she's all muscle. Her short black hair is fanned out behind her like a wet cockatiel. She's beautiful.

I smile and shake my head. "Thanks for this, duckling. I kind of wanted to spend some face time with you and Hank. The restaurant wasn't exactly my finest hour."

Eppie shrugs nonjudgmentally and I follow her back to the truck, sidestepping her shouldered board. "Café Chichi wasn't exactly my scene either," she admits. "For Christ's sake, the girl is dead. Do we have to pretend we all like each other now she's gone?"

I look sideways at Eppie. "You feel it too?"

"Hells yeah," Eppie says, swinging her board down to rest against the truck. "Maggie girl was the glue that held this little shitbox together. I mean, I love you, babe, and Hank does too, but Dane and Edina? Just looking at them crushes my mellow, you know? Maggie made it work. That's all there is to it."

I lean my back against the side of the truck, the metal warmed by the sun. The marine layer's not so thick today, the sheets of mist already lifting up and away from the ocean.

A hundred yards out, beyond Hank and his waiting board, a couple of dolphins wheel by. I point them out and Eppie grins. "My sisters," she says. "We play sometimes."

I think about my sister. Maggie. The only one there ever was.

Eppie hops up into the back of the truck. "You want a drink?"

"Sure."

She tosses me a can of orange soda from a cooler. "Sorry, out of caffeine."

"No problem," I say, and wipe the rim with the hem of my suit.

A moment later, Eppie emerges. "You don't usually take us up on the surf, girlie. So, what brings you to Mother Ocean this fine day?" She plops down on the back bumper. I join her. Eppie tucks her legs up to her chest, resting her arm on one knee. She drags a clove cigarette out of a pack on the floor of the truck.

"Want one?" she asks. I shake my head. "Yeah, me either. I quit months ago, but what can I say? I love the smell. They're not as strong if you don't light 'em, but still. Gives a girl something to do." She alternates between holding the cigarette between her lips and swigging her soda. We perch there, watching Hank beat the ocean into submission one wave at a time, punctuated by the occasional laugh from Eppie, who keeps an eye on her man.

"What brings me here is the same thing that brought me home. Maggie Kim," I say. *My Maggie.*

Eppie gives me a glance and shakes her head. "Man, I knew you were close, but you weren't, like, in love with her or anything, were you?"

I smirk. Me in love with Maggie. The idea. "I loved her, sure," I admit. "But I wasn't *in* love. Last I looked, you didn't have to be a lesbian to want justice for a dead friend. And you don't need to be screwing someone to want to understand why they died."

Eppie holds her hands up in a mea culpa, cigarette and soda dangerously clasped in the same hand. "Hey, hey, no offense. It's just, you came on kind of strong last night and had old Tallulah's panties in a bunch in nothing flat. And I see the way you and Edina give each other the stink eye. Maybe *you* didn't want to bonk Maggie, but I'm not so sure about that one."

She takes a fake drag off her cigarette. "She was stealing Maggie's clothes, you know. One piece at a time. I recognized them. Maybe it wasn't a sex thing, though. Maybe she just wanted to be a Maggie Kim impersonator."

For an instant, I can see it, a stage full of drag queens dressed in Hepburn black and Onassis veils, all smoking filterless cigarettes. Edina Rodriguez is at the end of the row, failing to be statuesque or convincing.

I laugh out loud and Eppie grins. "Jeez, I was wondering

how far I'd have to go to get a rise out of you. There were midgets in the next scenario."

I bump her with my arm. "I remember why we're friends now," I say, and she grins even wider.

"Cool. Say, I know Maggie being gone is, like, crazy and all of a sudden. That same kind of 'I just saw her yesterday' bullshit people always say. It don't seem right." Eppie shakes her head. "But Maggie had kind of a death wish about her, you know? She could party hard, and she could be a princess. She . . . I don't know. She could seem like she didn't give a damn. I'm not saying that's a reason for suicide, but maybe the drugs and an accidental bath in the family pool isn't such a surprise."

My laughter is gone, all dried up in that instant. "I never said it was a surprise. Maggie could have died a million ways to Sunday since I've known her. Just not like that."

Eppie is silent for a moment. I let the silence stretch, waiting to see if she's got something to fill it.

Eventually, she does. "Let's surf."

The ocean is cold, especially this early in the morning with the sun not quite hot enough to warm us, but we paddle out anyway, Eppie on her longboard, me on the shortie she and Hank keep in the truck.

I haven't surfed in ages, but it's like riding a bike. I know what to do. Paddling out past the break on my stomach, my arms are tired before long. It feels good, though. Being in my body instead of my head.

My lips are salty when I lick them. I sit up, straddling the board, and turn to face the shore. Nothing worth catching is rolling our way. Eppie sits a dozen yards to my right, bobbing like a rubber ducky. She's half water elemental, Eppie is. The ocean sings to her and she dances to the music, waiting for the crescendo. She waves at me. I smile back.

Up ahead, the small swells roll in, barely cresting white and washing up the pebbled sand. Hank is up shore from us and way out. We wait and I start to doze again, little waves rocking beneath me, lulling me to sleep. The sun comes out from behind a cloud and I close my eyes. Waiting.

"Sleeping pills," Maggie said.

"Running car in a locked garage," I countered. "You can't smell carbon monoxide and it puts you right to sleep. Pills you can always barf up."

We were sitting on the hill behind school again, at the start of junior year. There'd just been an assembly for some freshman who offed himself by hanging. Popular rumor said it was some kinky sex thing gone wrong, but students that knew the kid said it was only a matter of time. Maggie and I didn't know him, but it had sparked an interesting conversation: If you were going to do it, what was the best way to die?

"Old age," she said, and we both laughed. "Although, I guess that's not suicide. That's just life."

"Oh, I know. Death by chocolate," I said. "Definitely."

"The cake kind or the ice cream kind?"

I thought about it. "Both. I mean, you want to be sure."

Maggie snorted and we fell silent, suddenly feeling guilty that a skinny little fifteen-year-old was dead by his own hand, and we were celebrating life on his grave. We both sighed and watched the kids below us head for the buses or their cars, scattering across the parking lot like marbles dropped on a sidewalk.

"I'd want to be asleep for it," Maggie said finally. Like death really was the Grim Reaper and she'd rather keep her eyes closed than see him coming.

"Make it relaxing? Like lying on a mattress on a pool in the sun," I said.

"Like that," she agreed. The best way to die, when old age and chocolate just wouldn't do.

"Jude!"

Eppie's voice pierces my ears like the scream of a seagull. I'm in the water, floating, the surfboard tethered to my ankle slaps the surface beside me. I open my eyes. Eppie is there, suddenly, reaching, pulling me up from the sun-warmed water.

"There wasn't a mattress," I say out loud, and seawater fills my mouth. I sputter and try to help as Eppie pulls me back onto my board and frog-kicks us back to shore.

"I'm sorry," I say when we hit the coastline.

"Sorry? One minute I'm catching a wave, next thing I look back and you've rolled under. Jesus, I thought you'd whacked your head on the board and gone down," Eppie gasps.

We hit the strand and stumble, collapsing onto the sand. I feel half asleep. Like the song says, "life is but a dream."

We climb up the beach in slow motion, dropping our boards by the truck. Eppie reaches into the cabin for some towels and tosses one to me. I wrap up in it and watch her fish around for another clove cigarette.

"I'm sorry," I say again. "I was just thinking." *About Maggie.* But that much is obvious.

"Listen," Eppie finally says when she catches her breath.

"I know you guys were friends and you spent a lot of time together, but I think one of the reasons Maggie had such an odd lot of us was because she used us differently. I mean, there were things she could talk to you about that I would have been clueless on, and vice versa. So maybe you don't have the whole picture."

"And you do?" I ask.

She shrugs, shakes her head. "No. I don't. I mean, there are what? Seven other people to consider, including Hank out there. All I know is, one day Maggie asked me if I'd ever almost drowned. All the time Hank and I spend out on the water, sure, it's happened before. A lungful of ocean and that could be all she wrote. That's why we surf together and keep one eye on the water at all times."

"Why did she want to know?"

Eppie flicks imaginary ash from her unlit cigarette, both eyes on the ocean now, watching Hank as he comes in to shore and starts walking down the beach, board under his arm.

"She wanted to know if it hurt. God, I want to light this. I'd better . . ." She puts the clove in her pocket and tosses the pack away from her, into the depths of the Six-Pac. "She wanted to know what it would feel like to drown."

I nod. "Sleeping pills, a swimming pool, and an inflatable mattress with a slow leak. We used to talk about the best way to die. If the pills didn't kill you, the water would. And you'd sink down nice and easy."

Eppie laughs. "You don't know a lot about drowning. Not a pill in the world gonna keep the water from hurting when it gets into you."

I shrug. "Doesn't matter. We weren't going to do it."

Eppie doesn't look at me. "Yeah," she says, "right."

Maggie in the pool. Me in the ocean. I guess she's not convinced.

Eppie finishes her soda, belches loudly, and tosses the can toward a nearby trash drum. She makes the shot. Orange soda sprays around the inside of the garbage bag, rattling against the metal drum.

"So, it's just a coincidence, then?" She says it like she's asking a question. Or maybe making an accusation.

Eppie jumps down from the truck. Hank is almost here. She makes a show of helping him with his board.

"Hey, sleepyhead!" Hank calls out to me. He peels his wet suit down to his waist in that unselfconscious way guys who already have girlfriends do. It must be true love.

"Hey, Hank," I say back, and slide down so he can gain

access to the back of the truck. He disappears inside and Eppie and I are alone once again.

Eppie looks at me while I finish my soda. Then she takes the can from me and drops it into the trash with hers. "Joey's worried about you."

I shrug. "Everybody's worried about something."

"He really cares about you, you know. I thought you guys had something going there before school ended."

I feel my stomach tense. That's the problem with the past. No matter how much you might want to forget it, there's always someone there to remind you.

"Like what?" I say.

"Like *feelings*, maybe. We were rooting for you." She gives me a little smile.

"We?"

"Yeah. Me and Hank, even Maggie. You two deserve a little happiness. He's such a good guy, and you . . . used to seem kind of sad, when you first got here. But then you lightened up. You seriously think Joey had nothing to do with that?"

I don't know what to say. Maggie changed me. Maybe Joey did too, but Roy single-handedly changed me right back.

I don't want to think about this. I bite my lip to keep from answering.

"Anyway," Eppie says, giving up. "He likes you."

"Enough to come pick me up from Malibu?" I ask, ignoring the implication.

"No doubt." She shakes her head and finally lights her cigarette. Hank climbs back out of the truck, a granola bar in one hand.

"Break time's over, ladies," he says. "Let's hit it again."

"Not for me," I say. "I'm tapped out."

Hank looks at Eppie and shrugs. "To each his own. Blue House tomorrow night?"

"Definitely," I say.

He grins and winks at Eppie. "See you out there, babe." He kisses her on the lips and jogs back down to the water. I go inside and change back into my shorts. Then I text Joey. He can't stay mad forever.

He'll know if there was a mattress in the pool.

I sit down beside Eppie on the bumper when I come out. My phone buzzes with an incoming message: *No mattress. On my way.*

"What'd ya do, text him?" Eppie laughs. "God, he's whipped," she says.

"Maybe he just wants answers, like me."

"Well, I think it was suicide," Eppie tells me. "Maggie wasn't exactly happy, you know."

"I know," I say. "Still. You ever do a sleepover at her place?"

Eppie shakes her head. "No. Why?"

I smile. "Her suicides always ended with popcorn and a movie."

6

"You owe Tallulah an apology."

Those are the first words Joey says to me when I climb into his car at the beach. The top is down so we can wave good-bye to Hank and Eppie out on the water. They'll stay out here until the party tomorrow, then come back again after the funeral until school starts. I envy the simplicity of it all. The feeling they both have that this is home. But life is not that easy for the rest of us.

We pull out into traffic on PCH and wend our way back to Pasadena. The cars are moving a little faster headed in-land, but this is still going to take a while. We soak in the sun and the gasoline fumes, and I think about what Eppie said. Joey must really love me to sit in this crap both ways.

"Did you hear me?" he asks insistently.

But I don't give. "Tally owes the world an apology. She's a holier-than-thou colossal bitch."

"She's your friend," he reminds me.

"No. She's not. She's my classmate and my acquaintance. *You* are my friend. *Maggie* was my friend. Eppie is my friend. And Hank, and, hell, maybe even Lukey Loo, but not Tallulah."

Joey's knuckles tighten on the steering wheel. "We've known each other for a long time. All of us."

I sit back and put my bare feet on the dashboard. "Look at you, the peacemaker. Think about it, Joe. We all knew Maggie better than we know each other. She's gone now. 'Things fall apart. The center cannot hold.'"

Joey laughs sardonically. "Really, throwing first-year Yeats at me instead of admitting you're being petty? Tally's talking about skipping the funeral because of you."

"Oh?" I say, combing my fingers through my hair. "Who's being petty now?"

"Still you," Joey says.

"Hey, 'to thine own self be true.'"

My phone rings. I swipe it open. "Hello?"

"Jude, it's Dr. Bilanjian. How are you?"

The voice is female, neutral, calm, and oh-so-familiar.

It sends a jolt of adrenaline down my spine. "Dr. B," I say. "Long time no chat."

"Do you have a minute to talk?"

I look around at the traffic walling Joey's car in on four sides, the crowded beach to our right, the haze pressing down on us from the water. "I'm afraid not. I'm in the middle of something. What's up?"

Dr. B pauses for a long moment, lining up the words like golf balls on a practice range. Once she starts swinging, there'll be no need to stop. "Your mother called me. She told me she's worried about you and wanted to know if we could have a few sessions. Would you like that, Jude?"

Dr. Theresa Bilanjian is my psychiatrist. Not therapist, not counselor, my psych doctor. I am not on meds, nor am I in therapy anymore. But there was a time, right after we moved to Pasadena, when my mother thought a few months of talking to a professional would be a good idea. "To help you adjust," she'd said.

I'd gone to Dr. B for most of my freshman and sophomore years. By then, I'd made friends—namely Maggie— and I hadn't slit my wrists, so I was allowed to have my Wednesday afternoons back.

"Well, if you decide to," she says, plowing through my silence, "I have some time Wednesday afternoon. Why don't you swing by the office? It sounds like we'll have some things to talk about."

I hang there, mouth open, a thousand responses coming to mind, all of them negative.

"Okay," I say. The path of least resistance. If I refuse, my mother won't leave me alone. Dr. B is less cloying than my mom. "See you then."

"Who was that?" Joey asks when I hang up.

"Nothing. Friend of my mother's. Where were we?"

"Sitting in traffic, arguing," he says. We sit in silence and crawl forward a few more yards. I shove the phone call to the back of my mind. Dr. B can wait.

"Where are we going, exactly?" Joey asks, changing the subject. Good boy. Even I can use a halftime every now and then.

"Luke's. He's got something I need to see." Photos, I'm hoping. Scads of them.

But what would they tell me?

Maggie Kim was the sun in our universe. We all circled her. Never the other way around. And now that she's gone, we're shifting orbits. Colliding, like me and Tally, or drifting apart. It makes me wonder what Maggie saw in everybody else, these people she called her friends. Edina, Tallulah, Dane. What were they to her when they mean so little to me? And who meant so much to Maggie that she would share her bed with him, but not his name with the rest of us?

Or maybe he meant so little. And that's why Maggie's dead.

By the time we get back to Pasadena, it's nearly three o'clock, and later still by the time we get to Luke's house. Luke lives south of my place, in Alhambra. Craftsman bungalows and stucco apartment buildings swap blocks with each other, leapfrogging toward the boundaries of crisscrossing freeways. Luke's parents have money from a dry-cleaning chain they started when Luke was still in diapers. It keeps him in camera equipment and photography lessons. Soon it'll pay for a college education and maybe a portrait studio of his own one day.

The house is a stucco ranch affair, newer than the bungalows across the street.

Luke's father opens the door. "May I help you?" He's polite and looks like a professor, with his rolled-up shirtsleeves and rimless glasses. He speaks with a careful Mandarin accent. I wonder if he knows his son is a Class-A stalker.

"Is Luke home?" I ask. "We've got a photo project we're working on. He said to come by and he'd show us the contact sheet." Luke takes photography classes every summer. It's as good a cover as any.

Joey blinks at me but says nothing. Mr. Liu calls over his shoulder in Chinese. The distant sound of dishes being washed by hand stops and a woman responds. It must have been a very late lunch.

"Fine," a girl sighs in English. Amanda Liu, Luke's younger sister, appears in the doorway behind her father. He disappears into the house.

Amanda wipes her soapy hands on a kitchen towel. "Hey." She knows us from school, a freshman who's learned our faces the way a tourist learns major streets in a new town. "Luke had a thing. He should be back soon, though."

"Mind if we wait?" I ask. She hesitates, looks over her shoulder.

"How'd you like Shelstein's history class?" Joey says out of the blue. Amanda blushes and gives Joey a full metal smile. Her braces and her desire make me cringe.

"It was cool," she says. "Especially the Rome stuff."

"I remember that," Joey says, smiling a smile I've never seen. A confident smile. He leans into the doorway, posing pompously. "And that is why Rome wasn't built in a day," he says, mimicking Shelstein's gruff tones.

Amanda laughs and steps away from the door. We take the unspoken invitation and follow her inside. Chiming an explanation to her parents in Mandarin, she leads us back to Luke's room. The narrow bed is all but dwarfed by a desk with a giant computer monitor and a deep bookcase stacked high with photo albums and archival boxes.

"You guys want something to drink?" she asks, wiping her palms on her jeans.

"That'd be great," Joey says. He manages to make it sound intimate.

Christ, if this girl had a tail, it'd be wagging.

"Water," I reply.

She nods and scurries away. I drop down at the computer and start searching the photo files. Joey sidles up behind me. There's a stack of DVDs labeled for the past month on the desk, but none for the week Maggie died. It must still be on the hard drive somewhere.

Amanda comes back with two glasses.

"Oh," she says when she sees me on the computer.

"No, it's okay," I tell her. "Luke called my cell. He's running late and told me where to find the stuff. We'll just take a look and talk to him later."

Joey steps up and takes a water glass from Amanda, closing his hand over hers. As if that was necessary. I let him handle it and go back to scanning the files.

Suddenly, there it is. I pull a flash drive out of my bag and download what I need—Thursday, Friday, Saturday's photos. I shut off the computer and turn around. Amanda is drinking my water and giggling at something Joey said. Jesus, he's fast. It must have something to do with lower-classmen. They're not immune to him yet. His brown eyes and that damned smile.

"Done," I say.

Amanda is reluctant to see us go, but she perks up when Joey says he'll look for her at school. Just a hello in the hallway would boost her street cred. If it led to an actual date with a senior, it would change the entire landscape of her social life. Joey just threw her a bone. Or maybe he's scratching an itch and he wants me to know it.

"Home, Jeeves," I say when we're back in the car.

"Quite," Joey says. "Quite."

The living room is empty when we get back to my place, but I can hear the TV on in my mom's room. She doesn't say anything as we go by.

Joey follows me to my bedroom. I lock the door and flip on my laptop. Joey sits on the edge of the bed, drumming his fingers on his leg.

"You going to call Amanda?" I ask, plugging the flash

drive in and flicking through its contents. I see him shrug in the reflection on my screen.

"Just doing my job," he says, and lies back on my bed, bent at the knees.

"And what's that?" The photos are loading. Jesus. Even Luke's thumbnails are saved in high res. I turn to look at Joey while I wait. He's staring at the dingy popcorn ceiling, hands folded behind his head like he's looking up at clouds.

"The usual. To serve and protect," he says.

"That your motto?" I ask with a smirk.

He sits up on his elbows. "Every sidekick should have a motto. A code to live by."

"Oh, so you're my sidekick now?" I ask, raising an eyebrow.

"Close to accurate," he says. "What else do you call someone who stands by your side and gets kicked?"

He studies me for a long moment. I don't look away. "You think you've been kicked?"

"Right in the head." He lies back down. "Why else would I help you steal somebody's private property and flirt with his sister to do it?"

"For Maggie," I say, turning back around.

The pictures are loaded. I set up a slideshow so I can see them fill the screen.

If he's got something else to say, I don't hear it. Maggie's smiling at me from the screen, that brilliant red-and-white smile turned deep, saturated into black and white and moody grays. She looks glamorous in these pictures, thanks to Luke's love of monochrome. She would have been pleased.

Taken from afar, there are blurs in the corners, rose leaves and tree trunks that tried to block the camera and failed. He must have moved around, looking for the best angle. Maggie in the foreground, the house behind her, the street. The taillights of an old sports car driving by. And then there's Maggie again, sitting by her pool, drink in hand, laughing on the phone. The time stamp reads 18:00:00. Maggie was alive at six o'clock.

"Holy shit," Joey breathes at my shoulder. "You weren't kidding."

"Nope. Luke's been photo-stalking Maggie for almost a year."

"Huh." Joey sits down again, leaning forward to watch the show.

Maggie hangs up. Drinks. Smokes, never quite looking at the camera. She scratches the inside of her nose. These are candid. She doesn't know Luke is there.

But then something happens.

Maggie puts down her drink. She stretches. She looks straight at the camera.

The next instant, she's smiling. She disappears into the pool house and emerges in the slip, a matching robe over it. Not pool wear. She's dressed for seduction.

Behind me, Joey gasps. The pictures judder forward. Maggie is pointing at the camera. Still smiling, she reaches out a hand. Crooks her finger. She's inviting him in.

The slideshow stops.

Luke Fucking Liu.

I remember the roses on the kitchen table. The ones that came too early to be for a funeral. But they were for Maggie anyway.

"Shit," I say. "Maggie popped his cherry. Would he kill her for that?"

Joey shakes his head, scrubbing his face with his hands. "Why do you keep saying that? Maggie died. She killed herself. She got drunk and high and she took a header into the pool. Even if it was an accident, even if she just slipped, there is no killer here. It's just Maggie's fault. She got stupid and she's dead. You never blame her for anything, Jude. Never. But now you have to. Anything else is just crazy."

He stops his ranting and stares at me. "Listen, I know

you're hurting. I am too. I went with this because I figured you needed . . . something. But Luke Liu isn't a
killer. There hasn't even been a crime! I can't do this with
you. I'm done playing games."

He stops again. Sighs. And then he leaves.

There's a tightrope you walk with some people. Too far
to the left, and you lose them. Too far to the right, and
they want more than you can give. Right now, the line
is thrumming with tension. I've got to focus to keep my
balance, and hope Joey can keep his.

I sit there for a few minutes, Maggie's photo beckoning
me in. Then I lock my bedroom door again.

Tomorrow night at Blue House, I'll talk to Luke. And
as for Joey, I know I've just kicked him again. But he's
loyal. He'll be back.

7

Tuesday, my mother takes the day off work. "I thought we could spend some time together," she told me over pizza last night. I guess Roy has to work, because it's just going to be the two of us. I get up early and walk to the coffee place around the corner, unwilling to face her without some caffeine and sugar under my belt.

The line is short this morning. I order a latte and a cinnamon roll, then shuffle down the counter to the pickup line.

"Hey, Jude."

I look up. At the counter, Keith Dunfee, Maggie's ex, is nursing an iced tea. They lasted all of twenty seconds sophomore year. After Maggie had slept with his big brother,

Scott. That was some kind of baggage. Nasty baggage, if the wrong person ever opened it.

I move around the line to join him. "How's it going, Keith?"

He shakes his head. His skin is gaunt beneath the summer tan, the dusting of freckles prominent. "Kind of rough, actually." He takes a sip of his iced tea. "Scott's back."

Maggie and Keith had been a long time ago by high school standards. He wasn't her type, just a B student with B-level charm, but he worked part-time at the local animal shelter, which made him more of an A minus in Maggie's book. Keith had been her attempt at a normal high school boyfriend.

But nothing was ever normal with Maggie Kim.

Scott was more of a stereotypical teenaged dreamboat— a hunky blond football player who worked at the equestrian center. He was also a soldier, and Keith's idol. Hell, Keith might've been glad to get Scott's hand-me-downs once he found out.

But maybe Scott had felt differently. Maggie was the last girl he slept with before leaving the country. Finding out she had moved on might be one thing, but moving on with his kid brother?

I take the seat next to Keith and face him. "You heard about Maggie?"

"Yeah. I know you guys were close." He watches his cup make a ring on the counter. "Sorry."

"Me too." I rest my elbows on the counter. "When did Scott get back?"

"Not soon enough to say good-bye." He turns to me. "She ever tell you she slept with him? The week before his deployment."

I nod slowly, alarm bells ringing in my head. "Who told you?"

"Scotty did. When I first started dating Maggie, my mom sent him pictures from the spring dance, and he thought I should know."

So much for motive. Scott was up-front and honest. Maybe it came with the uniform, a twelve-step plan for making amends while at war.

Down the counter, the barista calls my name to pick up my order. I ignore her. "How did that go?"

Keith smirks. "How do you think it went? I was pissed she hadn't told me. I mean, we weren't together or anything, so what are you going to do? It's not like she was a virgin. But she could've said *something*." He clenches and unclenches the hand holding his iced tea.

"So what did you do?" I prompt.

"I confronted her about it and she told me everything."

I frown. "There was more?"

He cuts me a look.

"It's Maggie. There was always more." He relaxes his grip on the cup and exhales. "She was Scott's pen pal. Wrote a letter to him every week from the day he left, even after we broke up. Real letters, too, not e-mail. Perfume and everything." Keith smiles. "Scott said it made him feel like a doughboy or one of those guys in World War II."

I spin in my seat, my mind doing a few revolutions of its own. Maggie had been keeping up with Scott all this time. Or maybe Keith was the hitch in their longer romance? Either way, it wasn't a stretch to believe he'd think those letters meant something more. If the soldier boy was back, maybe their reunion went wrong. Maybe Corporal Punishment had finally lived up to his nickname. "You think she was carrying a torch for him?"

"No, nothing like that. It was just . . . The military wasn't Scott's first choice, and when his assignment came up in Afghanistan, well, nobody really wants to go to a war zone, right? But every few weeks, he'd get this batch of letters smelling like flowers and all the guys would go crazy. It made him feel . . ."

I think of how it would have made me feel. How it *did* make me feel, every time Maggie turned her attention my way.

"Loved."

Keith considers it. "Yeah, I guess. Loved."

I can see the appeal for her, writing love letters to a man in uniform. But why keep it from me?

A sour taste fills my mouth. I swallow and ask the question anyway.

"Did she say anything in her last letter to Scott?"

Keith wipes his mouth on his sleeve. "You mean like, 'good-bye, cruel world'?" He laughs. "No. She knew Scotty was coming home. It's got him messed up, making it back in one piece to find out she's gone. The last thing she said to him was 'see you in July.' To be honest, that's why I don't think Maggie killed herself."

I could hug Keith for saying it, for agreeing with what I've known all along. "So what do you think really happened?"

He sighs and rubs his face with his hands. "Scotty used to go on patrol every few days with his team and they always made it back somehow. But then, one day, there's this random helicopter crash and two of his buddies are killed." Keith takes a sip of his drink and fixes me with a look. "The majority of accidents take place within five miles of home, right? Cosmically, it sucks, but it's true."

"Is that how they comfort you in the army these days?" I say. "With statistics?"

Keith slides down off his stool. "Come on, Jude. We're in high school. We're like salmon swimming upstream. It'd be a miracle if we all survived."

I stare at him. "Seriously. You're comparing us to fish."

Keith smiles sadly. "Not everyone makes it to twenty-one." He rubs his eyes. "When's the funeral? Scott and I'd like to be there."

"Thursday. I'll send you the details."

He comes closer and gives me the hug I've been holding back. "See you at the funeral."

"Yeah. See you then."

He pushes the door open and a gust of heat rushes in to fill his place.

8

There you are, honey." My mom is waiting for me at the kitchen table when I return. A stack of fashion magazines is fanned out on the gold-and-white Formica and her car keys are in her hand. "I thought we could get breakfast, but I see I'm too late."

"Sorry, jet lag. I couldn't sleep," I lie, and toss my empty latte cup into the trash. My mom frowns, but pulls it up into a smile.

"That's okay, hon. It's your day. What would you like to do? I was thinking mani-pedis?"

I look down at my bitten nails and decide to throw her a bone. "Sure. I know a place at the mall. They give facials too."

"Terrific," she says, shuffling the stack of magazines. "I got these for you. I thought you might like them."

I don't read fashion magazines.

I come up with a smile. "Thanks," I say, taking a seat at the table across from her. "I spoke to Dr. Bilanjian yesterday."

The magazines stop moving. "Did you?" My mother tries to watch me without looking directly at me. "What did she have to say?"

"She said you were worried about me and wanted to make sure I was okay."

My mother crumples with relief. "I am, honey. You're going through a rough time, and we don't ever seem to talk like we used to." She reaches across the table. "I wanted to make sure you were handling things okay."

I pull away. "Mom."

She drops her hands to her lap and takes a breath. "You're still my daughter, even if you aren't a little girl anymore. You just lost your best friend, honey. Don't you want to talk about it?"

I study the sparkle pattern in our old Formica table, a retro constellation of glittering gold. The girl I used to be was close to her mother. The girl I used to be would date a boy like Joey, get her picture taken in the front yard before prom, and live on the East Coast with a mommy and a daddy and a stack of beauty magazines.

Do I want to talk? "Yes," I say, and I can feel her expanding with the joy of being useful.

"But not with you."

Sometimes, you open your mouth, and out comes nothing but knives. It's happening more and more with me these days. I should talk to Dr. B about that. When did my default mode become "bitch"?

Was I this way before Maggie, or only after Roy?

The bubble pops and my mother looks away, blinking damp eyelashes. Maybe Maggie's mom was onto something. Looks like I'm going to Hell, too.

"You're not the first person to lose someone, Jude," my mother says. "And you won't be the last."

"Every high school has a body count. Yes, I know. Thank you for telling me. You're the second person today."

My mother glowers at me. "Why do you have to do that? Can't you see?" She's trembling, red-faced, a matchstick about to catch light. "I'm just glad it wasn't you."

And there it is. I love my mother. And I kick myself for not being able to show it. Because she still loves me, even if she sucks at it sometimes.

She slaps the tabletop with the palms of her hands and stands up, grabbing her keys in one fluid motion, like a kid playing jacks. "Now, I'm going to get my nails done. Are you coming?"

The trip to the nail salon turns into a condolence visit to the Kims when my mother's little tirade reminds her of her neighborly duty to drop by. I take the opportunity to scratch an itch that's been nagging me since Edina cornered me in the john.

When Violetta answers the door, I head around back, to the pool house.

Maggie's pain-in-the-ass brother, Parker, is sitting on the terrace in his high-backed wheelchair, staring at the roses. Behind him, through the French doors, I can see my mother joining a sofa full of mourners. Better her than me.

⸻

"Parker's in the hospital again." Maggie delivered the news in a neutral tone. Like directions to the nearest post office, a common destination devoid of any emotional drama.

"Oh?" We were on the phone, so I couldn't read her face for clues on how to react.

Parker had been in and out of the hospital since he was eight years old, when the tumor squeezing his brain like an accordion was finally big enough to show up on his pediatrician's radar. Every so many months, he went in for tests. Occasionally it was for longer, more complicated surgeries to shift his skull plates around and make room for his unwanted tenant.

"Mommy Dearest and Father Knows Best are beside themselves again," she continued, and now I could hear the sigh over the phone.

Maggie didn't hate the disease that was slowly killing her brother—there was no point, it couldn't be changed. And she didn't hate Parker, even though he was the sort of self-centered prick who would merit it. She understood: being a favorite case study of world-renowned surgeons with God complexes can make you a prick from a very young age. She didn't even hate the extra attention Parker got from the 'rents or the medical set.

She was Maggie Kim. She grabbed plenty of attention on her own.

What she *did* hate was how her parents handled everything. They'd go crazy whenever Parker was due for a new test, never mind a new surgery. Relatives came to town. Concerned friends. Her folks milked the overwrought parent act for all it was worth.

"It's like a practice wake over here," she told me. "You should see the way my mom looks at me, like it's my fault

I'm healthy. I swear, if Parker could've been fixed with a brain donation, my mom would've sliced me up for spare parts ages ago." She sighed. "I actually offered once."

"Offered what?"

"To take his place. I was, like, eight. Parker was so scared, and they were all walking around like he was already dead. So I said I'd get the surgery instead."

I stifle a snort.

"Don't laugh. I meant it at the time. Dumb kid that I was. And you know what she said? 'I wish you could.'"

We were both silent for a moment. "Well, you did offer," I said.

"I know. But that's kind of shitty, right?"

"Yeah. But your parents suck. That's nothing new," I said.

"Oh, you want new?" she laughed morbidly. "This time, my mom's found religion. There's a minister. In my house. When he showed up with his little congregation of professional mourners, that was the last straw. Come over and help me. I'm moving into the pool house."

———————————————————————————————

I skirt the edge of the swimming pool and raise a hand to block the sun. "Hey, Park and Ride," I say.

From his spot on the terrace, Parker doesn't bat an eye. "Fuck you, Jude. Good morning."

I can't help but smile. Maybe it started as jealousy over Maggie, but I've come to enjoy our little sparring sessions. "Did you know every high school has a body count?"

Parker is a sophomore in the world of the home-schooled and tutored. He's a high school on wheels.

"Do tell," he says, but he's not looking at me. He's staring at the roses, white and frowsy, petals falling to the ground like snow. I've interrupted a private meditation.

"I'd have put my money on you," I say. But he still doesn't look up. From this angle, even with those black-rimmed glasses in the way, I can see the parts of him that look like Maggie. I clear the sudden catch in my throat and turn away. "Just came to pick something up."

"And you can see how much I care."

I almost laugh. His voice sounds as gruff as mine.

I open the pool house door and step inside. Nothing has changed. I go to the bookshelf where Maggie kept a shoe box full of photos, the ones she bothered printing, and the ones so old they were developed at a drugstore a century ago.

I perch on the sofa with the box in my lap and shuffle through the stack inside. Luke Liu would wet his pants if he knew this was here for the taking. And he can have it, as far as I'm concerned, minus one little photo I don't want Edina's filthy little eyes on again.

What started as a quick shuffle slows down as I flip through Maggie's former life.

There she is in the dress she wore for the spring dance, back when Keith was still her man. And the two of us, punked out for Halloween. This box is like a time machine, drawing me backward. There are pictures from before I ever knew Maggie. One with her whole family on what must be a vacation in Korea, judging from the signage behind them. She's a skinny kid with a glossy bowl cut, standing half hidden by Parker's wheelchair. And an even earlier one, back before the wheelchair and the surgeries, when Parker was just a little boy. Brother and sister huddled on the doorstep of this very house back in its prime, the two of them grinning as the Popsicles in their hands run red and orange onto the ground like finger-painted sunshine. On the back, Mrs. Kim's flowing cursive lists their ages: Maggie, 7, Parker, 5.

I touch the photo. Maggie's brown eyes sparkle back at me. The bowl cuts, the sugar-stained smiles. She and Parker could almost be twins.

I close the box. Whatever Maggie did with my picture,

it isn't here. Just one more mystery she'll take to her grave.

Parker's missing from the terrace when I leave the pool house. I make it back to the car just as my mother opens the Kims' front door.

She shuts it carefully behind her. "That was hard," she says.

"Tell me about it."

She gives me a tired smile and climbs into the driver's seat. "There but for the grace of God," she says.

Translation: Don't kill yourself, Jude.

She doesn't have to worry about that. The two of us have already been plenty of places where angels would fear to tread, and I haven't done it yet.

"Did you know Maggie got into Brown?"

"Yeah, early admission."

There's a headache starting behind my left eye. I don't want to talk anymore.

"Such a bright girl," my mother says.

"Like the sun," I agree.

My mother's lips twist as if she's keeping something clamped down. She thinks I'm being sarcastic, bitter.

Good guesses. But I mean what I say.

I slump in my seat. The pain has moved to both my eyes.

"I saw you outside with Parker," my mother says. "How's he holding up?"

I shrug. "Parker is Parker."

"This must be hard for him," she says. "I know they were close." Which goes to show how little she actually knows.

Start the car, I think. *Just start the car.*

Instead, she turns and looks at me.

"What about you, hon? How are you feeling?"

I close my eyes against the ache in my brow, my temples, rising up the back of my neck.

"I'm fine," I say, opening them again. "Let's just go."

She sighs. One of those deep, loin-girding exhales that I've grown so used to. It's the sound of tolerance. "You don't sound fine."

"Please," I say. "I have a headache. Just . . ." I mimic her sigh. Like mother, like daughter.

Another twist of the lips.

She turns the key in the ignition, and pulls out onto the road.

9

July is going out in a blaze of glory, and the fires have marched from here to Malibu. All across the LA Basin, the sunset is gory with smoke and a deep red haze.

Eppie and I stand on the bluff at the edge of Blue House's backyard and watch the sky over Eagle Rock dim into night. Behind us, Hank's band is playing something fast and guitar-filled, wordless and loud, bouncing their sound off the back wall of the house. Blue House leans to the left as if it's dancing, a two-story drunk of a clapboard shack painted every single shade of blue. Eppie's dad bought out the remainders at a paint store years ago. Whenever the wind and sun strip the wood of color, he slaps on another layer.

I had to ask my mom for a ride here tonight. She loved it. After pre-manicure weirdness and a lunch chaser, it was yet another chance to "participate," as the counselors call it, to play the supportive parent. She didn't even mention a curfew, bless her heart. Just said to call her when I was ready to come home. It was easier than chasing after Joey. He's around here somewhere. Just not around me.

Eppie clacks her plastic cup against mine and I can smell the alcohol spiking her 7Up. I'm a water-over-ice girl, myself, but I like the way the booze rises warm and sharp off Eppie's breath. It makes me feel like someone else, like we're both other people in another place that's not quite so fucked up.

"Here's to the simple things," she says.

"Tic-tac-toe and algebra." We hoist our glasses and drink.

"Still mooning over Maggie?" she asks me after a second sip.

I look out at the moon hanging low and bloated in the eastern sky. "Is that supposed to be a pun?"

Eppie grins. "Naw, girl, just a question. I'm worried about you."

"I know. But don't be. I'm a big girl."

"Yeah." Eppie drops the grin. "But so was Maggie."

"What's your deepest, darkest secret?" I ask suddenly. It's been on my mind since seeing Keith this morning. I'd been so sure my best friend shared everything with me. But she hadn't.

If I'd thought about it, there were lots of little hints, morsels of secrets surrounding her, like crumbs from an earlier meal. Sure, she'd told me about Dane the minute it happened, and I thought I knew about her own dalliances, up until Luke. But there was Scott, who used to want her, and maybe still did, despite what Keith believed.

And what was it Edina had asked me the other night? *Did she ever talk about me?* She hadn't, not really. Or maybe I just hadn't asked.

Eppie flinches. "Wow. That's a big question. And we're not even high. I don't think I can answer that."

"You *can't* answer, or you won't?" I ask.

She looks at me for a minute, no longer laughing it off. "Won't. It's none of your business."

I nod. "Fair enough. But is there anybody you *would* tell?"

Eppie takes a long time to answer. When she does, her drink sits forgotten on the lawn and she shivers as she says it. "Maggie. Maggie knew."

I laugh and I know it sounds bitter. "Yeah, she was the

one I told too. It's like the end of the King Midas fable, the guy with the golden touch that kills everything he loves? There's another myth where he's punished with donkey ears. He keeps them hidden under his crown, but someone catches him with his ears out and Midas swears him to secrecy. But this guy can't keep a secret that huge, so he runs out into a field, digs a hole in the ground, and shouts into the hole, 'The king has the ears of an ass!'" Eppie smirks at that, but she's listening. "So he shouts his heart out, then fills in the hole, burying the secret, or so he thinks. Over time, reeds grow over the hole, and when the wind blows hard enough through them, it sounds like they're saying 'The king has the ears of an ass!'"

Eppie starts laughing outright and I join her because it feels better than making my point. But, when the laughter stops, she asks me, "What's that got to do with anything?"

"Maggie. We all told her our secrets, every single one of us. And now we're filling in the hole. What do you think the reeds will say when the wind blows?"

Eppie smiles, then frowns, attempts another smile and fails. "It's just a story, and not a very good one, Jude. It doesn't make sense."

"Maybe we just have to be listening," I say.

Whatever happened to Maggie, she might have been

telling us all along, and I'd missed it, mistaking it for so much wind.

So I tell Eppie another story, this one not so old.

_____

"How many months before you start to show if you're pregnant?" Maggie asked.

We were lying out by the pool again, our perpetual California pose. Towels draped on lounge chairs laid flat for sunbathing and catnaps.

I peeled open an eye. "Five months? Maybe four if you're rail thin, or six if you're tall?"

Maggie sat up, looking at her mother's roses. Explosions of white and pink flowers made the upper terrace look like a French dessert.

"How far along can you be and still get an abortion?" Her voice was neutral, matter-of-fact, but I could hear the strain in it. It was the same voice she used when she talked about Parker's surgeries, careful not to care.

I turned to look at her—almond skin, perfect hair, perfect body. Her stomach was as flat as her voice.

"Three months."

Maggie looked at me. "And you know this why?"

I pulled on my sunglasses and shrugged. "You're the one who asked. I know things."

She snorted, then looked alarmed. "Sweetie, you weren't . . ." She petered out like a vapor trail of concern.

"Knocked up?" I asked, eyeing her over my shades. "No. My aunt miscarried a few years ago. She was four months along and I couldn't tell she was pregnant. I got curious and looked it up. And the abortion thing is . . . bonus-round trivia. Late-term abortions, women's rights . . . Don't you watch the news?"

Maggie lay back down on the lounge chair. "It's bad for my complexion."

"Right."

We were silent for a while. The cackle of wild parrots filled the warm Saturday sky. Legend had it a pet store burned down and those were the escapees, a mass of feral noisemakers thriving in the not-quite-tropical desert air. But the truth was there were several of these colonies all over Southern California. That's a lot of pet stores burning down for no good reason.

I looked up and caught a flicker of green and yellow in the distance. They screeched and clacked like geese in a box of castanets before flying on to another berth.

"Why do you ask?" I said in the descending quiet.

Maggie grimaced, a flash of white teeth, lipstick vanishing into a thin line. She shook her head. "I'm a little slutty, Jude, but I'm not stupid. Parker got the genetic short straw this time, but any child of mine could turn out to be partly cloudy with a chance of tumors too. Who needs that at seventeen?" She sighed. "Besides, there *are* other people in the world. People I'm concerned about."

"Anyone I know?"

"Can we ever really know anyone?" she parried.

I softened my tone, giving in. "Sure. I know you, Saint Margaret, patron of lost causes."

The tension left her shoulders and she gave me a wry smile. "I think that's you, dear. Saint Jude."

I had to laugh. "I *am* a lost cause," I agreed.

Maggie grinned. "That makes two of us."

Eppie gazes down at the city lights.

I'd taken a chance—maybe she knew something I didn't. Maybe Maggie had been pregnant and depressed and I'd missed all of it. Because I'd needed Maggie Kim to be invincible and sure of herself. Because she was my shield from the world.

"I saw Keith this morning," I continue.

Eppie sounds far away when she says, "Oh, yeah. He and Scott couldn't be here tonight. How are they?"

"He's fine, but I hear Scott's a mess. He had a thing

with Maggie. I thought it was over. But maybe it wasn't. Then I remembered, he was home on leave last year when Maggie started asking me those questions, and it kind of made sense."

"It wasn't Maggie," Eppie tells me. "Not everything is about her."

She's so quiet, I can barely hear her. I lean in, pulling up my hood to block the sounds of the party. The music is loud, out of place here on the edge of the world. "What?"

The sky tilts as I try to rack focus from one story to another. Eppie. Not Maggie after all.

She takes a deep breath, and when she speaks, it's like she's pulling water from a well deep inside her. "It was spring break. Hank and I went down to Mexico to surf Rosarito right after his grandma died. He was having a hard time and we wanted to relax, take a load off for a while." She laughs nervously and pulls out another clove cigarette. "Mexican condoms," she says, and shrugs. "It was . . . tough, Jude. I mean, we love each other, but we're kids. We just couldn't have handled it."

A real friend would have known, or guessed. But Hank and Eppie had been drama-free in my book and I've been tearing out every page that doesn't say "Maggie." I've seen so much, it's hard to admit I've been blind.

"I didn't know," I say.

She shrugs. "Nobody did. Except Maggie. I went to her for advice. I guess she just seemed more worldly than the rest of us."

"Did she help?" I ask, thinking of how little Maggie really knew, how she had come to me in turn.

But Eppie nods. "It always helps, to have a friend listen. But it was still hard. Very hard." She shakes her head, remembering. "Say, don't bring it up with Hank, all right? He doesn't need to go through it again."

I hear the reprimand in her words, even though she doesn't say it. He doesn't need to relive it, but neither does she.

"I won't," I promise.

Eppie is one of the last good ones. She deserves to be happy. I'd hoped that was already the case, but she had me fooled.

Now I'm starting to wonder if Maggie was the only real innocent in our circle, or did she have other secrets of her own?

"Why are you digging this up, Jude?" Eppie asks. She sounds angry and defeated and sad.

I take her hand in mine. "Because ever since Maggie died, I've felt alone. I'm starting to see I'm not the only one."

Eppie looks at me then, really looks, and I wonder what she sees. Someone like Scott who can't let go? A delusional girl with a death grip on the past? Or a friend? She squeezes my hand.

"Do you know why I went to New Jersey?" There were a few reasons, but I would only share one. "To see my dad. On neutral ground, at my aunt's place."

Eppie shifts positions, trying to follow the change of subject.

"It was . . . bad when my folks split up. I haven't seen him in four years," I explain.

Eppie relaxes. This is quid pro quo. Secrets are better shared, so I'm giving her one of mine.

"How'd it go?" she asks. The spotlight is on me now. She breathes deeper. I don't. But I keep going.

"It didn't. Maggie died before I could see him. And she's the one who encouraged me to go."

Eppie's face crumples with dismay. "I'm sorry, babe. That sucks."

"It's fine," I lie. "He's remarried. Some woman with a daughter my age. They sent me wedding pictures after the fact. A surprise elopement to an island somewhere. I guess you can't get there from LAX, or they'd have asked me to come. Right?"

Eppie is giving me soft eyes. "That's bogus," she says.

"Yeah."

We sit for a moment in raw silence. Quid pro quo's a bitch.

"You're not getting too heavy over here, are you?" It's Eppie's dad, Mike, come to check on us.

Mike has an easy way about him that's a thousand miles distant from my own parents. I can imagine my mother at this party if she'd stayed, voice pitched too high, tottering around in inappropriate shoes for a barefoot, flip-flop night. She'd be oh-so-friendly to everyone while they laughed behind her back. My dad would just sit in his car, dialing the cops.

But Mike takes a swig from his beer and says, "Come on, Shasta's reading cards." He reaches out a rough, weathered hand and pulls me to my feet. Eppie waves good-bye and steals the chance to recover herself while I follow Mike through the crowd.

Tallulah and Dane are here. She's perched on his lounge chair like a teacup on the edge of a shelf. Dane lazes back, a drink in one hand, the other playing with her hair. I've seen it before, the Appearance. She's counting the minutes until she's been here Long Enough and can leave. Dane's got his hand on her and his eyes on the girls dancing near the fire pit. He looks like a lion in a cage, each stroke of her hair like the lazy swish of a tail.

I follow his gaze through a mosh of blond- and red-haired girls from school, and spot Luke Liu on the far side of the fire. He's drunk. It doesn't take more than a look to know it. He's in his uptight Windbreaker with the unironic '80s Nehru collar over a polo and pressed jeans, but there's a bottle in his hand and his face is red the way some Asian people get with their inability to metabolize alcohol quickly.

Maggie never turned red. She'd had too much prac-tice, or better makeup.

I wave, but Luke doesn't see me, his eyes intense and watery, glaring into the flames of the pit, as if daring the fire to stand up and fight. No point in questioning him to-night. I doubt he can string a sentence together, let alone a coherent thought.

I wonder where Joey is.

A twist, a turn, and Mike pulls me inside the house to-ward the sunroom that backs onto the yard. Outside, the heathens leap and thrash to Hank's music. Inside, there's a short line for the bathroom and the telltale scent of pot seeping from under a closed door down the darkened hallway. A sharp giggle verifies the illicit goings-on.

That's the thing about Blue House: Mike doesn't judge. Hell, it's probably his stash.

Shasta is sitting on the old plaid sofa that faces the French doors as we enter. For an LA girlfriend, she's surprisingly age-appropriate for Mike. A weathered, sun-bleached blonde in an Indian-print caftan and shorts, she's got the cards laid out before her in a Celtic cross, a cross pattern of six cards, four down the side. Tiffany Green, one of the girls from my French class last year, is staring at the cards, wide-eyed with the spiritual insight she's just received.

"That's so freaky!" she exclaims. "I . . . Wow, freaky! I'll have to think about that! Thanks!"

She rises unsteadily, bringing a plastic cup with her, and shakes her head as she stumbles out the door.

"Milady," Mike says, and urges me toward the sofa.

"Hey, Jude," Shasta greets me, and scoops the cards into a pile again. "Shuffle and ask away," she says, handing me the deck.

I tap the cards into shape, but I don't shuffle, not knowing what to ask.

Who killed Maggie? Why did she die? Will I be pretty or rich? And what would it mean if I got an answer, anyway? Nothing that would hold up in a court of law.

Seriously, Your Honor, a fortune-teller told me the butler did it.

"Oh, boy," Shasta says. She's good at reading more than just tarot cards, apparently. She takes the deck away from me and picks up both of my hands in her own.

"You poor, poor thing," she says. She turns my palms faceup and rubs her thumbs over them. It would be creepy if it wasn't so soothing. "You're not ready for answers, kitten," she tells me. "It's just too hard right now. I know what that's like. People die and you're left there looking for a reason. Poor thing," she croons again.

I feel a sigh building in my chest. I look at the cards on the table. I should ask a question. Just a simple question.

Suddenly, Shasta stops rubbing my hands. She squeezes them tight and looks at me earnestly. "Do you want to get high, hon? It might help."

"No, thanks," I tell her, and try not to shake my head at the kindness of hippies. "But don't let me stop you," I add.

She doesn't. She leaves me on the couch, staring at the cards. I flip over the one on top of the deck. It shows a picture of a man in a tunic with a hobo bindle over one shoulder, a dog at his feet, about to traipse happily off a cliff. Beneath the picture a caption reads "The Fool."

But the card is upside down. I'm going on a journey, and I don't have a leg to stand on.

A sudden movement in the window catches my eye.

Outside, by the fire, Joey has joined the dance.

"I'm glad you're not here all summer," Maggie said to me. She blew a smoke ring from her stinking Ukrainian cigarette and adjusted her sunglasses with a painted fingernail.

We were decked out in swimsuits and cutoff shorts, cleaning out pitchers in the sink of her pool house, prepping them for a second batch of teenage hangovers and regrets. I washed while Maggie dried with one lackluster hand and smoked with the other.

Outside, in her parents' backyard, half the student body was partying, drinking spiked lemonade and strawberry daiquiris made from a cheap mix. Her parents and Parker were gone for some weekend church retreat and school had just let out for the summer.

Next year, we'd all be seniors, masters of our universe. Maggie bought the vodka and let us splash in her pool, we provided the rest.

"I'll miss you, too," I said back.

"Don't be a dolt. I'm gonna miss you, but you're lucky.

You see all those fools. Mark Draper just did a cannon-ball. Jesus. Does anybody do that anymore?"

"Apparently Mark Draper does."

Maggie pulled down her shades to fix me with a look. "That's what I mean. This is the future of America, Jude. We're college-bound and pathetic. Most of these guys are just looking to skate into UCLA or a CSU somewhere." She looked out the window and shook her head. "Seriously, we're killing off brain cells just looking at these idiots."

"Well, you have summer school, don't you?"

Maggie was infamous for taking extra classes at Pasadena City College every summer. I didn't know why. She still sat next to me in AP English each fall, but it made her feel cosmopolitan, as she put it.

"Do you see what I mean?" Maggie said, drawing deeply on her cigarette, then flicking it into the sink. I listened to it sizzle into a wet cinder beneath the soapsuds. "You get to go back east. I have to go to fricking PCC just to talk to anybody who isn't a troglodyte."

"Hey, I'd be happy to hang out all summer. Me leaving was your idea."

"Yeah, well, not telling your mom about Roy was yours. Leaving is the next best thing."

To running, I wanted to say. When things got bad in my

family, my mom ran from my dad. I didn't want to be like her, but there I was, packing to go.

"You need to work some shit out, Jude. See your dad. Curse him out, or give him a hug—whatever it takes. You can still hook up with Joey next year. He'd look good in a tux."

"Prom? Really?"

Maggie sighed. "You're seventeen, Jude. Live a little." She looked out the window and lit another cigarette. "I'll try to do the same. Even with this lot."

She wasn't wrong. It was my turn to sigh. "Well, these are *your* friends," I pointed out.

Maggie wrapped an arm around me. "You're my friend. Joey's my friend. Dane, Tally, Eppie, Hank, Edina. With a handful of exceptions, the rest are just"—she waved her free arm around me, her silver bauble bracelets clashing with the gesture—"extras. And not very good ones at that. Jesus." She pointed out the window just in time for me to see Mark Draper dive back into the pool and lose his swim trunks.

"Charming," Maggie drawled.

I laughed. "We are truly blessed."

"Come on," she said. She yanked off her bikini top and dropped her shorts on her way out the door. "Let's show them how it's really done."

It took me a second to follow. When I did, my clothes stayed on.

Blue House after midnight. Out in the yard, kids are drunk and dancing, or slipping off to make out. I go splash some water on my face in the suddenly empty bathroom, and wander back outside.

I want to go to sleep, but not here, and not at home. The thought of calling my mother to come get me is repugnant, so I return to my perch overlooking the city and wish I had a vice. Ice water and memories do not an Irish wake make.

But Maggie was my vice. All my bad habits and rash decisions balled up into one beautiful girl. She would have danced around the fire, and I would have watched her, laughing. She would have taken a hit from Shasta's little glass pipe, still cold from the freezer, and not even coughed. She would have walked up to Joey and put her arms around him from behind and said, "Take me away from here," and he would have seen it as a seduction, a rescue. An apology.

But I'm not like Maggie. I never was.

I pull out my phone, and dial home.

10

I'm not good for much the next day. I wake up with a headache pounding the back of my skull, and a scream in my throat. I miss my life before this weekend. I miss Maggie. Her death hangs in front of me like a weighted curtain I'm powerless to lift.

It's early, my mom and Roy are still asleep. It was a big night for her, picking me up from an actual party. The house is quiet.

I lie in bed and stare Death in the face. A tear streaks down to my pillow. My hands clench.

I'm sick with anger, with the need to turn back the clock, to erase eternity. Orpheus went to the underworld to snatch back Eurydice. Superman flew backward around the earth to resurrect Lois Lane.

Me, I sit up, slide my legs out from under the covers, put one foot on the floor, then the other, and will myself to stand.

I pull some clothes from my dresser, and shuffle down the hall to the bathroom. I turn on the shower and take a long hot piss while the water warms up. When I flush, the water pressure from the showerhead dips. This is wildfire season and our plumbing is sympathetic to the needs of the fire department.

I step into the shower, head still beating like a drum, and feel the water on my face like tepid tears. I turn it up as hot and strong as it can go, hoping to scour the pain away, to feel something on the outside instead of this burning futility within, but as I said, it's fire season. The water sputters rather than blasts, and gets no hotter than a cup of vending-machine coffee.

Maggie's funeral is tomorrow. I need caffeine and something black to wear. That means the mall, or Maggie's closet.

Mrs. Kim said I could have anything. The pearls are already around Edina's undeserving neck. But there's a certain dress and hat that might still be waiting for me.

I climb out of the shower. Pull on my shorts and a tank. Grab a Diet Coke from the fridge for breakfast.

Fortified, I head out the front door, my spare set of Maggie's pool house keys in hand.

═══════════════════════

"I think it's sexy."

"I think you look like a widow in a bad movie," I told her.

Maggie stuck her tongue out at me from behind the black birdcage veil she was wearing. "Tally and I picked it up in NoHo."

God knew there were enough thrift stores and costume resale places around this city for the two of them to play dress up for the rest of their lives. "Tally's a poser. She dresses like a Connecticut housewife."

Maggie turned to me and vamped, hips thrust out at an angle, one hand thrown back in a casual fake laugh. The black sheath and pumps made her look like Jackie O, complete with pearl choker.

"I think she's got style," she said. "Tally's traditional. She's just growing into it."

"So, in another twenty years, the twinsets and pearls will make sense. But her boyfriend will still be a pretty-boy jackhole. Like I said, poser."

Maggie clucked her tongue and struck another pose. "Dane's not so bad, really. They're kind of like Beauty and the Beast."

"But who's who?" I snarked. "Mags, seriously, ditch the hat."

Maggie adjusted the pillbox on her head, humor fading. "Are you kidding? I'd rather go naked, like Godiva, *avec chapeau.*"

===

I step outside my house. Joey is waiting for me on the curb, an extra-large latte in each hand. I could kiss him. But I have my pride.

Maggie once told me Joey tamed a wild squirrel with bits of food and a safe place to rest in his backyard. Eventually, it was eating out of his hand. But wild is as wild does. One day, it bit him, and that was that. I hope I don't do the same thing.

I leave my unopened soda on the front steps.

"You didn't say hello last night," Joey says.

"I thought you weren't speaking to me."

"Maybe I would've. If you'd said hello."

We look at each other for a moment. In the light of day, he's got shadows under his eyes. Just like me. I almost laugh. That's the thing about parties—everybody looks happy.

Everybody's lying.

I step closer and say, "Hello."

He hands me one of the drinks wordlessly and we climb into the car.

"Maggie's," I say. "Then Luke's."

"Your wish is my . . ." He lets the sentence hang.

I reach out and squeeze his hand. We don't let go until we get to Maggie's.

The hat is there but the dress is gone. Who says you can't take it with you?

"We gave it to the funeral director to . . ." Mrs. Kim's hands flutter around her face like pale butterflies. "Oh, I wish I had known you wanted it."

"No, it's perfect," I tell her, and ask to keep the hat.

"Certainly, certainly," Mrs. Kim says, already looking around for something else to do or say. "There was one thing, though. A strand of pearls. They were my mother's. She gave them to Maggie before she died."

The words hit hard and Mrs. Kim sits down suddenly on the couch. Burying her daughter with her dead mother's pearls. Sometimes the circle of life is more of a noose.

"Edina has them," I say, sitting beside her.

Joey stands in the living room doorway like a bodyguard.

"Edina? Who's Edina?" Mrs. Kim asks.

Joey and I exchange a glance. I shrug. "Another friend. Maybe Maggie gave them to her?"

"Ha." Mrs. Kim laughs derisively. As if Maggie might have done it against her express wishes, to hurt her. Maybe she had.

"I could be wrong," I say. "If they turn up, I'll let you know."

For a moment, Mrs. Kim looks paler than usual. "The . . . the coroner called today."

Joey leans forward. I stiffen. "Oh?" The strain in my voice is obvious.

Mrs. Kim shakes her head, staring at the pattern in the carpet at her feet. "I don't understand it. They say they found drugs in her. Did she do drugs?"

The look she gives me is so raw with grief that my voice catches in my throat.

When I clear it, she's still waiting, begging me for an answer. "No, Mrs. Kim," I say. "No, she didn't do drugs. She never touched them." It's the sort of lie you tell a mother. Aside from pot, it's also the truth.

"Then how did this happen?" she asks. "Valium, they

say, Vicodin, Rohypnol. Where would that come from? Where would she—" She breaks off suddenly, remembering something, or overwhelmed with grief, and in an instant, Mrs. Kim the starlet is back. Placid, poised, impossible to read.

"Mrs. Kim?"

She looks at me for a moment, her emotions brushed off like so many flies. She pats my leg. "Thank you, dear," she says. "I've got the service information in my office. Let me get it for you." She rises and totters off, looking old.

"That's hard-core," Joey says. Even he's surprised.

Maggie didn't do drugs like that. It has to be a mistake.

"Note to self," I tell him. "Get a closer look at the coroner's report."

"So, I'm your secretary now?" he asks.

"Nope. You're my better half."

"Vicodin, Valium, roofies." Joey recites the litany of drugs found in Maggie's system.

We're back in his car, headed toward Luke's house. As we head south, the thin, curving palm trees give way to sheltering magnolias again. Joey's eyes flick from the road to me and back again.

"Date rape drugs," I point out. "And everyone thinks it's a suicide?"

Joey shifts uncomfortably behind the wheel. "We call them date rape drugs, doctors call them relaxants. I guess a lot of people OD on the same stuff when they're trying to off themselves. Mrs. Kim didn't say anything about . . ." He hesitates to say it. "About rape."

I take off my sunglasses to rub my eyes. The wind and pollen have dried them out. "Maybe the Kims would rather have a suicidal daughter than a raped and murdered one."

Joey shrugs. "But wait. If Luke had drugged her for sex, why would she dress up for him? Wasn't she going to sleep with him anyway?"

I don't like it, but he's right. "Unless it wasn't Luke."

"Maybe," he says, but I know he isn't buying it.

"Besides, if it was suicide, where did Maggie get the drugs? I mean, she sometimes smoked pot, and she tried ecstasy once. But roofies and Valium?"

Joey turns to look at me. "You're kidding, right? Between Mrs. Kim's nerves and Parker's brain tumor, I'd bet there's an entire pharmacy in that house. Valium and Vicodin would be easy."

"Which might explain Mrs. Kim's adept change of subject. But roofies? What are those, a marital aid?"

Joey turns onto a side street, shaking his head. "No. I don't know about those."

I take off my glasses again, wishing we had put the top up. "Well, maybe Luke Liu does." I wipe my eyes. The trees are wreaking havoc on my allergies. Magnolias stretch out before us, a cocoon of glossy dark leaves and creamy white flowers enveloping the never-ending road.

We find Luke in Central Park, south of Green Street, thanks to a tip from a blushing Amanda. I've got to hand it to Joey—he knows how to work the younger ones. When he knocked on the door, all it took was a sheepish smile and she practically wrapped her legs around him.

Luke is photographing the empty playground like a pedophile planning an assault. He frowns when he sees us crossing the dying St. Augustine grass and turns back to arranging his shot. When we're close enough, he lowers the camera and faces Joey down.

"I know you came by my house the other day. Leave my sister alone, Joe."

Joey raises an eyebrow, looking more surprised than threatened. "The way you left Maggie alone?" he asks.

Lukey Loo blanches and fidgets with his camera. Pale

as he is, his cheeks turn deep red. "I never did anything to Maggie," he says.

"No," I agree. "More like, she did it to you. Or is it more PC to say you did 'it'"—I use air quotes—"together?"

Luke hunches over like he's going to be sick. "Oh God, oh God. You saw my photos. That's why you came over that night? Just to . . . I . . ." He stops, hands resting on his thighs.

"Sit down, Luke," I tell him. He nods and finds his way to a nearby bench. Joey and I join him.

Luke takes a few hiccupping breaths and pulls it together. Almost.

"When you asked . . . about it at dinner, I couldn't say anything. It would seem like bragging. But it wasn't like that. It . . ." He looks up at me, pleading. "You don't speak ill of the dead." He swallows, sits up straighter. "It wasn't the first time she offered."

Joey and I exchange a surprised look.

"She . . . Well, I always said no. I just took pictures, watched over her. If we were ever going to cross that line, I wanted it to be real." He shakes his head. "I'm not stupid, you know? Maggie was a tease. She was a slut maybe too, but I loved her. That's why I . . ." He falters, and gestures with the camera. "I wanted her to be safe. But I'm human and the one time I give in, I let her send me home afterward."

"You said she'd offered before," I say. He nods numbly. "So, why take her up on it this time?"

Luke swallows hard. "If you saw the pictures, you saw that car pulling away? That was Dane. Maggie said he was thinking of breaking up with Tally, even though he loved her. You heard the rumor he'd been cheating, right?" His eyes flick to me and down again. "Well, yeah, you heard, because of that thing you said at dinner. Anyway, I guess it was true. And he didn't think he'd ever stop."

"So why'd he go see Maggie?" I ask.

"I guess they talked about that kind of stuff. I don't know. But Maggie thought it was brave or something. Romantic. She said she'd never had that with anyone."

"Had what?" Joey asks, looking to me. *A cheating boyfriend? A guy who would dump her?* I shake my head.

Luke shrugs his narrow shoulders. "You know. Love."

He looks lost for a moment, pulled back to that night. "But then there was me. One-sided, but love just the same. There had always been me." He slumps in on himself. "If I hadn't slept with her, maybe she wouldn't have . . ."

"Killed herself?" I say. "She didn't."

He stares at me, a flicker of relief turning to confusion.

"But . . . even if it was just an accident . . . if I hadn't left, maybe she'd still be alive."

After Luke gets through with his blubbering guilt trip, he agrees to help us re-create Maggie's last day.

"I've got other pictures from that night. Or at least, I will."

"What did we miss?" I say.

Luke wipes his nose on his sleeve, eyes still glassy, and refocuses. "I'm working on a new series of slides. It's not like regular film, or digital. The grain is fantastic and the black and white can be really intense." He's in his realm now, a different person. Confident. Excited.

Maybe that's what Maggie saw in him. All I ever saw were the puppy-dog eyes and the camera.

"It needs special processing," he explains. "Stuff I can't do in my dark room at home. So there's a place I go in Hollywood. I dropped it off the next day, before . . . before I found out about Maggie."

After he'd already ordered the flowers, I'm guessing. I can see it, lovestruck Lukey Loo drifting down the side-walk, cupids and hearts floating around him like some sap in a 1940s cartoon, off to get the pictures printed from His Big Night.

Every kid should have snapshots of his first time.

Something to remember it by. And something to brag over later. Which might be true for most teenaged boys, but not Luke. For him, it was high art or nothing.

"When can you pick them up?" Joey asks. It's a foreign concept to me, sending out canisters of film and waiting for prints. The sort of thing my mother used to do. There are still little black-and-yellow rolls of film in the corners of our closet, waiting for someone to care enough to see what's inside.

"Tomorrow. I can call you when it's ready."

"Perfect." I rummage around in my bag. "That reminds me, Maggie's mom gave me the funeral info." I find the Post-it note in my purse. The details are already in my phone, so I hand it to him. Any confidence he was feeling shatters and he breaks down again. I feel bad, but it's getting late and grief is private, so I hand him a few more tissues and Joey and I leave him to it. We've got a mall to shop.

Paseo Colorado is more the idea of a mall than the real thing. Here in Southern California, where malls are outdoor temples for sun worshippers with discretionary incomes, the Paseo is a soulless construct. Except for the classy ArcLight theater and a couple of oddities like the antique mall, it's your grandmother's shopping center: a big anchor store and a few bland chains.

We come up the escalator from the creamy white parking lot and out into the sun.

"Joe, grab a coffee," I say, and take the long walk into Macy's. I haven't shopped here since junior high. This is the kind of place mothers go to clothe their families for holiday parties and special occasions. Funerals count as special.

I flip through three sales racks and a few designer clotheshorses before I find a suitable match. Another fifteen minutes in the dressing room and I've settled on a sleeveless sheath dress with a lace overlay, black on black. I pull Maggie's pillbox hat out of my bag and check myself in the mirror. Jackie O all the way.

On the way out, I stop at the costume jewelry counter and buy a twenty-dollar strand of pearls.

"Ready?" Joey asks, shoving an iced mocha toward me. He's soaking up the sun at a café table for two. I drop my purchases and sit beside him.

"Yep." I suck down a dram of mocha and feel myself relaxing for the first time since I got home.

"Where next?" he asks.

I pull out the necklace and let the luminous beads spill across the palm of my hand. "Edina's, of course."

Edina lives in a small apartment building just north of the 210 at the edge of Altadena. As the name implies, Altadena sits above Pasadena, with its back up against the towering San Gabriel Mountains. Once a genteel place of bungalows and Italian firs, now the city is just Pasadena's homely little sister.

Edina's mother smiles at us from the front doorway of their three-unit cottage apartment and shakes her head. "Eddie's not home," she says in accented English. "YMCA."

Joey and I get back in the car.

Apparently Edina's got a summer job. She's a lifeguard at the community pool. Imagine that.

We walk out onto the deck of the Olympic-sized swimming pool surrounded by a fifteen-foot chain-link fence. A stern guy in a pair of regulation red-orange trunks and a white Y camp T-shirt tells us to sign in and take off our shoes. We sign the clipboard, kick off our flops, and march across the pebbled ground to Edina, sitting at the end of the pool.

Maggie could pull off a one-piece suit, but Edina has

the added challenge of the Y's color—she looks like a misshapen tomato and she knows it. She catches sight of us and wraps a thin towel around her waist. It doesn't help.

"What do you want?" she asks.

"Maggie's necklace. Her mom wants it back."

Edina scowls. "I don't know what you're talking about."

I sigh. Joey looks bored. "Little pearl number. The choker from the other night. Family heirloom, sentimental value," I tell her.

Edina's scowl falters. "But . . . Maggie gave it to me. She knew I loved it. She said it was mine."

"When was that?" I ask.

Edina looks lost. Her fingers go to her throat, to a choker that isn't there.

"The . . . the day she died. I went over to pick up some stuff she was donating to the camp—old beach towels and whatnot." Her face hardens. "Bet you didn't know that. She was charitable, your bestie. Even volunteered with the toddlers sometimes."

I shrug. "I wasn't her keeper, Edina. Just her friend."

"I feel sorry for you, Jude," she says. Her eyes flick from me to Joey and back again. "For both of you."

If that's bait, I don't take it.

"Can we have the necklace, or do you want to tell her

mother no? Funeral's tomorrow at noon. I'm sure she'd love to meet you and hear all about it in person."

Edina opens her mouth, then shuts it again.

We turn and walk away. I smirk and Joey nudges my arm. "Don't," he says.

"Don't what?" Now I'm full-on smiling.

"Don't enjoy this too much," he warns me. "When it's all over, you won't have any friends left."

I wonder if that includes him.

11

Mrs. Kim calls me in the middle of lunch with Joey. They want me to help finalize the funeral plans.

She hopes I haven't already eaten. I lie around a mouthful of French fries and promise to be there by two o'clock.

"What was that?" Joey asks when I hang up.

I wash down my fries with a swig of soda and wipe my mouth. "Lunch at the Kims' in half an hour."

He drops his burger onto the plate. "Are you kidding me?"

I shake my head. "We're going to talk funeral plans. Favorite music, flowers, and such. The final touches for the big day. Don't worry, you don't have to come."

Joey looks relieved. "Seeing them at the funeral will be awkward enough," he says. His worry passes and comes back pointed in another direction. "You sure you're up for that?"

I look at my fingers on the table, and drum them against the laminate top. "What would Maggie do?"

He smiles and puts his hands in the air, index fingers pointing up. He spins them in circles and we both say, "It's a party!"

"What do you think happens when you die?"

Maggie was high on pot and introspection the night of her grandmother's funeral.

"Coroner picks you up, or a funeral home. Then there's a funeral and they bury you. Or cremate you." I shrugged. "Then everybody eats."

Maggie laughed coughingly. "Very spiritual. I mean, what happens to *you*, not your body. What happens to your *soul*."

I blinked. We were on the back patio of her parents' place at two o'clock in the morning, long hours since her mother had cried herself to sleep in her husband's arms.

Parker had a procedure scheduled for the morning, something to reduce pressure on his brain. The tumor was growing, along with the strain on his family. It was just rotten timing that his grandmother chose that week to die. The Kims always got circumspect and quiet before a Parker surgery. And Maggie always got high.

She and I were the only conscious people on the block that night. A perfect setting to talk about eternity.

"The Buddhists say you get recycled," I told her. "And the Christians think you go to Heaven to hang with God. And Jesus."

"Become an angel," Maggie said dreamily.

"Yeah, maybe."

She exhaled long and slow like she was still smoking, although her joint was finished before I even showed up.

"What do you think?" she asked. I shrugged again. "Is there a Hell?" she pressed.

I looked down at my feet, still in their flip-flops despite the cold, my robe tied tight over my pj's. "I hope so."

Maggie laughed, a mad cackle. "That's a stupid thing to hope for. What if you end up there, frying like a fricking weenie roast on Satan's big old stick?"

We both laughed at the obscenity of the image, and I swatted her arm for good measure.

"That was blasphemy," I said. She kept laughing, waggling her fingers and eyebrows in a Groucho Marx imitation.

"No," she said. "That's entertainment."

"Maybe that's all we can hope for." I raised an imaginary glass to the cold, starless sky. "Whatever lies in the great beyond, may it be entertaining."

Lunch *is* a virtual party at the Kims' place. A genuine catered affair. A chiseled twentysomething guy in a white shirt and black apron smiles at me from the depths of the kitchen as Maggie's father ushers me in.

"That's Bruce," Mr. Kim says, introducing Apron Man. "From Sunset Café. They're catering the reception after the funeral. We're tasting the menu today." He pauses, runs a hand through his clean-cut salt-and-pepper hair. "Thank you for coming. We should have asked sooner. We appreciate your input."

"Not a problem," I say, and follow him out back to the patio. Someone has turned on the misters and a fine spray of cooling water evaporates overhead, just shy of our sun-baked skin.

Mrs. Kim wears a pair of pearl earrings that, no doubt, were a matching set with Maggie's missing choker. The pearls complement her latest facial and the linen sheath dress she's wearing. Mr. Kim looks country-club sharp in pressed khakis and a pale pink polo. Sprawled in his

high-backed wheelchair, Parker glances at me from behind his black-rimmed glasses. He's dressed all in white:
white polo, white shorts, buttoned up and proper.

I feel underdressed for the spread before me, food and
family alike.

Dropping my bag, I take the seat across from Parker,
straightening my tie-dyed tank top as I go. "Hey, Parks.
How's it rolling?"

Parker sneers at me, then turns it into a smile for his
folks. "Terrific," he says. "I'm finally an only child."

"As nature intended, no doubt."

Maggie's mom is staring hard at the cloth napkin
twisted in her lap. She's never scolded Parker a day in his
life—why start now? Mr. Kim clears his throat. "Try the
salmon, everyone. I'm not sure fish is a good idea for a
buffet on a hot day, but it looks delicious."

"Maggie hated cold salmon," Parker says, but his
father isn't listening. He dishes out plates of the stuff—a
whole poached fish on a platter surrounded by carved
vegetables—then goes on doling out the other dishes as
Bruce the Caterer whizzes in and out of the house, adding
trays to the spread. Poor guy. Two misery meals for the
price of one. I'd rather stick a toothpick in my eye than
serve the Kims twice.

"So, Parker, were you home on Friday night?" I ask.

He shrugs. "Hmm, I don't recall having brain surgery that day, so either I *was* home, or I should fire that surgeon."

"That's a good one, Parker." His dad laughs and turns to me. "His therapist says humor is a good way to deal with his illness and emotional stress."

I nod. I wonder if his therapist knows the difference between humor and sarcasm.

"What do you think?" Mr. Kim asks suddenly. "Of the food, I mean."

"It's delicious. Go with the curried chicken salad and cold roast beef. The antipasti with extra mushrooms, and maybe that fruit spritzer. Maggie would approve. But Parker's right. Skip the fish."

Parker gapes a little. Here I am, agreeing with him, and the sky hasn't fallen. I never imagined he and Maggie were close, but he obviously knew her better than his parents did. He catches my eye and, for a moment, I can't look away.

Mrs. Kim breaks the silence, looking both flustered and pleased. "Oh, thank you! She's so efficient, isn't she?" she asks no one in particular.

Parker yawns. "I'm not hungry," he says. "I'm going

to my room." He presses the joystick on the arm of his wheelchair and maneuvers himself away from the table, but Violetta isn't here and the doors aren't automatic.

"Good luck with that," I say with a wink. The jab feels good after the weight of his eyes on me. Maggie's eyes.

"Why not take a swim?" Parker replies, rolling toward the doors regardless. "I hear the water's nice."

As if summoned by an invisible bell, Violetta appears and pulls the sliding glass doors open for His Highness. He flips me the bird with a lopsided smirk and wheels past a flustered Bruce, laden with miniature brownies on a silver platter. Bruce deflates when he sees them leave. "No dessert?"

We finish lunch with Bruce's fudgy brownies and coffee to the sounds of Parker groaning his way through a physical therapy session with Violetta in his room.

Mrs. Kim selects "Amazing Grace" as the hymn and we agree on a casket spray of long-stemmed bloodred roses. The funeral plans finalized, I say good-bye to Maggie's folks and take the long way out through the yard.

I stop in front of the pool house, by the row of lounge chairs running from the door to the far end of the water. Parker's quiet upstairs. I look up at his bedroom window on the second floor at the back of the house, tucked under the eaves of three-layered Spanish tile. I can just see Violetta folding a towel through the closed window. She turns around, sees me, and waves. I wave back and look at where I'm standing.

Joey found Maggie's body by standing here. Parker's room had a direct view of Maggie's demise.

I change my mind about walking out the long way and exit through the house.

By the door sit a few pairs of shoes, Mrs. Kim's small Coach purse, and a larger messenger bag. Violetta's. I take a look inside before slipping quietly out the front door.

12

W hat's up?" Joey pulls up to my house just as I round the corner on the long, hot walk back from Maggie's.

"Hey, sidekick. Didn't think I'd see you so soon," I say.

He climbs out of the car. "Tally's definitely not going to the funeral."

"Why not?"

He comes around the side of the car, scowling at me. "She and Dane broke up, just like Luke said. You still owe her an apology."

I shrug. "Their breakup has nothing to do with me. All the sorrys in the world won't make Dane keep it in his pants."

Joey folds his arms across his chest. "But it might make her feel better."

I drop my bag to the sidewalk and look him over. "Why, Joe? What's it to you?"

He looks past me, avoiding eye contact. "When your parents split up, what did it feel like?"

I blink, taken aback. "What?"

Joey sits down on the hood of his car. "We've got one more year together. Just the eight of us, now Maggie's gone. I'd like to spend it with friends. There's time enough to be alone in college."

I study his face, unable to tell if he's being honest or not. Joey's always been a bit sentimental. Maggie's death must have pushed him overboard.

"Fine," I say. "On two conditions."

He nods, listening.

"One, you also take me to see Dane."

Joey laughs, but agrees. "Sure, he deserves an apology too."

"And then, you listen to what I have to say, and you help me with one more thing."

Joey gives me a look. "Sounds like three conditions, but fine. I take it you learned something at the Kims'?"

"Yeah. The Sunset Café makes fantastic brownies. And Parker was home the night Maggie died."

"So?"

"So, his room gave him a front-row seat to her drowning."

Joey's eyes widen. "What are you getting at?"

"I'm not sure. But did you know that nurses keep a log of patient activities while they're on duty? They have to share it with the supervising doctor and prove their billable hours to the home health agency."

Joey nods slowly. "Fascinating," he says in a way that means it's not.

"I got a look at Violetta's log from the day Maggie died and the day after," I continue.

"And?"

"And they're missing. Skipped over or torn out, I couldn't tell. She's already keeping a new book, even though there's a week's worth of pages left in the old one."

He hesitates. "And what does that mean?"

I smile. "It means that the health agency is about to get an angry call from Mr. Kim for being overbilled. He'll complain Violetta didn't work those days and they'll pull out the logs to prove it. He'll demand to see them for himself, of course. And then we'll know exactly what Parker was up to when his sister was drowning outside his bedroom window." I tap a finger against Joey's chest. "You do have a fax machine at home, don't you, 'Mr. Kim'?"

Joey grabs my hand, trapping the offending finger. He's

trying not to laugh. "You've really thought this through," he says.

"I have."

"Okay. Tally first, then the fax."

I sigh. "Agreed."

Tallulah stands at the top of the curving stairs in her parents' debutante ball of a house. She's wearing a bathrobe, too posh to be anything but designer, and there are tissues falling out of the pockets. Her nose is red.

"Don't come any closer," she says down to Joey and me in the foyer. We loiter beneath a crystal chandelier and tuck our hands behind our backs so as not to frighten her off. When she sees we're not storming the castle, she relaxes a little.

"I'm sorry. I just have this awful cold and I'd hate to spread it to anyone."

Joey and I successfully avoid looking at each other. If she and Dane are split, she's not sharing for some reason.

"Want us to bring you some soup?" I ask.

Tallulah hesitates, almost coming down the stairs a step. "Thanks, Jude. Really. That's nice."

I shrug and look around. Tallulah's house is a contractor's idea of the antebellum South. In addition to the chandelier and curving staircase, there's an honest-to-God Juliet balcony outside, running the entire facade of the house, covered in wisteria vines. Inside, the feeling is reflected, literally, in long paneled mirrors that face the tall windows on either side of the front door. *Posh* is too small a word to describe it. *Tacky*, however, is not.

"So . . . what's going on?" Tallulah asks. Awkward conversations can be made even more awkward by a flight of stairs, it would seem.

"We just came to see how you were doing. And . . ." I look at Joey and he nods me forward with a thrust of his chin. "And I wanted to apologize for the other night. I was out of line. Losing Maggie . . ." For a second, I have to choke back an honest sob. Saying the words makes the pain sharper. "I don't know. I guess I wanted everyone to hurt. But of course, you were her friend too. So, I'm sorry."

Tallulah backs away from the top of the stairs, terry-clothed arms folded across her chest, half hug, half disciplinarian.

"Yes. Well." She might not have a cold, but her voice has turned downright icy. "I'm sure we're all very sorry. But news flash: actions have consequences. Maybe if Maggie knew that, she'd still be alive and Dane and I . . . and Dane." She stops, holding back tears.

"You deserve better than Dane," I say.

The look she gives me is pure venom. "Really? And you would know? Honestly, Joey, I don't know why you puppy-dog around this little tramp. She wouldn't know love if it hit her in the face."

Joey steps forward, but I cut him off. "If it hits you in the face, it ain't love," I say, echoing a conversation with Maggie from long ago.

Tallulah goes very still, and I wonder if Dane's been rough with her.

"God, Jude. You and Edina and your fucking hero worship. What? You think I don't recognize a Maggie impersonation when I see one?" She takes two steps down the stairs toward us, both hands clutching the railing like an invalid.

"Maggie killed herself, Jude," she says emphatically. "And you're acting like she was better than that. She wasn't. Maggie Kim was a cliché. 'She seemed so happy. Had everything to live for.'" She makes air quotes with one hand before gripping the banister again. "There is no prize for surviving, unless you have a life. And some of us do, Jude. We have lives. Something to get back to when our friend is in the ground. Dane and I . . ." Here she loses her cool. Tears edge into her tirade and her voice cracks. "Dane and I had each other, until you went and pissed all over it."

I start to respond, to tell her that one little snipe on my part does not a breakup make. They were together at Blue House, after all. But Joey squeezes my arm and I keep my mouth shut. This is Tallulah's close-up. I let her have it.

"Poor little Jude," she says. "You're the only one who's ever been hurt."

She sounds like my mother. Maybe they would get along.

I glance at Joey to make sure he's seeing this. I'm being good. I've bitten my tongue, but now it's starting to bleed.

On her high horse, Tallulah sighs. "Maybe . . . maybe Maggie had the right idea."

"Tally," Joey says, starting toward the stairs.

She holds up a hand to stop him. "I'm not suicidal, Joe. I'm tired. Don't you ever just want it all to stop?" She runs a hand through her long chestnut hair. "I'm going back to bed. Shut the door on your way out."

"Will do," I say.

Joey hesitates a second, but I'm already walking away. The front door and the door to Tallulah's room slam at the same time.

"Jesus," Joey says, putting his sunglasses back on. "That went well."

Suddenly, I wish I smoked. One of Maggie's cheap Ukrainian cigarettes might make me feel better right now. Like I didn't care.

"That, my young friend, is why a lady never apologizes," I quip.

Joey raises an eyebrow over the dark lens of his shades. "Lesson learned," he replies. "Um, what she said back there about me. I'm not puppy-dogging you."

I don't look at him. "I know."

"I'm just . . ." He loses momentum. I wait. "Holding on to the people I've got," he finishes.

And now it makes sense. It's what Tallulah meant. When you bury someone you love, you need a life to return to, or you just might not make it back to the world of the living.

Joey found Maggie's body. He doesn't want to see any more death. Not even the death of a friendship. When Luke broke down in front of us, he cried like a baby and didn't care that we saw. But not Joey. He's just been holding it in for everyone.

I take his hand. "You've still got me."

He smiles, just barely, and we head down the garden path back to his waiting car.

• • •

Dane lives on that part of the arroyo designated for old money. His mother is former Pasadena royalty, one of those girls on the Rose Parade floats waving with their flashing plastic smiles.

Joey pulls up. We're the only car on the street. Everything else is privacy hedges and towering trees.

"Be right back," I say, and swing out of the car. I asked Joey not to come with me. Dane likes girls. He's comfortable around them. And stupid. Maybe he'll tell me something he wouldn't if Joey was there.

The driveway is like a private country road hemmed in with boxwood on both sides. I follow the curve until I see an eye-catching sight up ahead: Dane washing his car. It's the little sportster in Luke's pictures from the night Maggie died. Dane's dad gave it to him when he turned sixteen. Cherry red, a German import from the '60s. It's his baby.

He's standing over it with a garden hose in one hand, a chamois in the other. He's shirtless, tan, and toned. Behind him the house rises out of a bed of roses, ornate and Spanish. The terra-cotta roof shingles are stacked five thick, and rococo flourishes surround the peaked windows and wrought iron balconies.

"You look like the centerfold in a dirty magazine," I say by way of greeting.

Dane catches sight of me and smirks. He cuts off the hose, and continues to soap up his car.

"Ah. Hello. Come to snipe at me some more?"

I close the last few yards between us, standing just outside the puddle of water surrounding his pride and joy.

"Actually, I came to apologize."

Dane stops soaping. He tosses his sun-bleached hair out of his eyes. "Seriously? Can you say 'too little, too late'?"

I take a step closer. "I was sorry to hear about you and Tallulah."

Dane laughs bitterly. "Right, that's why you brought up gonorrhea. If I'd known you wanted me for yourself so badly, I would have complied. Tally wouldn't have needed to know." He leans back against the car and gives me a lascivious look, nailing his pinup pose. I laugh.

"Poor, poor little Jude," Dane says, uncannily echoing his ex. "You're so fucking miserable, and you want to drag the rest of us down too."

I've stopped laughing. "Fuck you, Dane."

"No, thank you." He smirks. "Haven't you heard? I like them younger."

"I thought you liked them on roofies," I counter. "Like Maggie."

Dane spits and goes back to washing his car. "Where did you hear that? I've done a lot of things, even some unforgivable ones. Maybe I've hurt Tally, sure. But not Maggie." He stops and faces me again. "As for the rest . . ." He spreads his arms, shedding soap foam as he indicates his body, his car, his house. "I'm Dane Hanover. I don't *need* roofies."

"Sarcastic clap," I say. "So, why'd you dump Tally?"

He shrugs, looking uncomfortable for the first time. "Who's to say she didn't dump me?"

"Tally's face, for one thing. She still wants you. And then there's Maggie. You went to see her the night she died."

Dane sighs and turns the hose back on, running a stream of water down the hood of the car. It gleams like candy-apple-red nail polish in the sun. "Yeah, I did."

"And you asked her for advice."

Dane gives me a sharp look. "How do you know that?"

"What did you want from her?"

Dane finishes rinsing the car before he answers. "Maggie kept me honest. If it wasn't for her, I wouldn't have told Tally about the other girls. If she'd found out some other way, she'd never have forgiven me. But I 'fessed up and she actually appreciated my honesty." He laughs self-consciously. "And here we are, coming up on senior year and I know, I just know, I'm not a one-woman guy these days. I didn't want Tally hurting, so I asked Maggie what to do. She'd been right the last time. She said, 'If you love her, but you can't be good to her, let her go.' I thought that was bullshit. You know, that 'If you love something set it free, if it comes back it's yours' BS that camp counselors used to say? I didn't listen. Then Maggie turned up dead, and you came home. Your . . . comment at dinner just underlined it. I love Tally, and I'm hurting her, so there. Finito, as they say."

I look at Dane, with his cosmetically perfect good looks, the studied boyish charm. The shallow jackass with the perfect life. He looks wounded. Not the sort of practiced look that makes gullible girls want to mother or make out with him. The tired sort that comes from a broken heart. I wonder if I'm seeing what Maggie used to see.

"I'll leave you to it," I say after a moment. I start to head back down the driveway when something makes me stop. There were reasons we called him and Tallulah perfect. In a lot of ways, they had been. For a while, anyway. "Dane?"

"Yo," he says nonchalantly, the armor already settling back into place. He's nothing if not resilient.

"I am sorry," I say.

He gives me a small smile, and I know he's thinking of Maggie when he says, "Yeah, me too."

13

This is unacceptable!" Joey bellows into his home phone. The number is unlisted. No chance of being called back.

Joey lives in a nice house—well, nice for 1963. My mom's little multi-lot cottage is no dream home, but Joey's place is strictly Brady Bunch, from the orange and avocado curtains to the mustard-colored sofa set in the wood-paneled living room. When your single parent is a dad, I guess redecorating falls by the wayside.

Joey's bedroom is a different story. White walls, black furniture, a glass desk. It's a New York City loft trapped inside a split ranch time bubble. It also has its own AC unit cranked to deep freeze.

I collapse on the black duvet and spread out, willing the hundred-plus-degree heat to leave my body while he rattles the folks at the home health agency. We've just caught them, fifteen minutes to closing. It's been a very long day.

"Taking advantage of my family while I'm away on business is the kind of shenanigan that will get you reported to the licensing board!"

I raise an eyebrow at "shenanigan."

Joey shrugs. He nods to the person on the phone. "No, I do not have a copy. Who's to say it wasn't falsified . . . signed by my wife, you say? Yes, you can fax it over and I'll take it up with her. This is why the account fell behind. The man that pays the bills is always the last to know. Yes. Certainly. One moment." He rattles off his fax number and hangs up. We stare at each other in the silence of the ticking house.

"Congratulations, Joey. In the history of crank calls, you win the Oscar for Most Eclectic Use of the Word 'Shenanigan.'"

Joey groans. "I choked. But it worked. And I found out something else—the bill's past due for the second time this year. You think the Kims are having money problems?"

I think about it—that great big house, but with the AC

turned off. Mrs. Kim always dressed like a country-club doyenne, complete with jewelry. Always the same jewelry, but always the best. And Maggie, with her imported cigarettes and massive wardrobe. She never seemed to hurt for spending money. "I don't know. Maggie never mentioned it, and I think she would have, if she'd known."

"Well, it's hardly the kind of thing her folks would advertise, especially to their kids." Joey shrugs. "Maybe it's a fluke. Some bills just fall through the cracks."

"But medical bills? Parker's their baby. They would never let anything get in the way of his care."

"Violetta's still on the payroll," he points out. "So it can't be the end of the world."

I frown. "It was for Maggie."

He scowls at me. "An elephant was born at the zoo last week. Does that have something to do with Maggie too? You're chasing shadows."

"And you're helping me."

He looks heavenward, shaking his head. "I'll get the fax."

Joey ducks down the shag-carpeted hallway to his father's office and returns with the home health agency's report. I half expect it to be printed on that flimsy ancient thermal paper, given the rest of the house, but the sheaf he holds up is crisp and modern.

"Got it." He pushes me to one side of the bed, sitting

down so we can look at it together. "Time sheet," he says, flipping past the first page. Violetta worked a long twelve hours the day Maggie died. Eleven a.m. to eleven p.m., with four of those hours being overtime.

The second page is an hourly log written in Violetta's tidy cursive.

11 a.m.—Patient returned home from PT session.
    Gave bath and massage.
12 p.m.—Patient napped.
1 p.m.—Patient ate lunch.
2 p.m.—Delivered afternoon meds.

The list went on.

"Flip," I say, and Joey turns to the third page. Parker eats dinner, gets his chair wheeled around the block for fresh air, and does his homework with a tutor.

"Even on a Saturday in the summer? That sucks," Joey says.

"No wonder he's such a prick."

Joey laughs and we turn to the last page, the final three entries:

9 p.m.—Patient in distressed mood. Argued with parents.
    Needs rest.

10 p.m.—Patient unable to sleep. Read book, watched TV.
  Still distressed.
10:30 p.m.—Patient requested anxiety meds. Calm,
  resting when I took leave.

The last page is a list of Parker's prescriptions. Vicodin and Valium are on the list, along with a few other words that read like sneezes—flunitrazepam, methylprednisolone, topiramate.

But no Rohypnol.

Parker was drugged and calm by 11:00 p.m. And Maggie was dead.

"That lets Parker off the hook," Joey says. "If he was sedated, there was nothing he could have done."

"It *is* a coincidence, though." I flip through the log. "He didn't need medication any other night of the week." I stare at the pages in my hands as if they can give me answers. But there are none that I can see.

"So, what do you think they fought about?" Joey asks.

"Money? School? Maggie? No idea."

"Violetta knows," Joey says.

I grin. "Think you can charm her the way you did Amanda?"

Joey cracks his knuckles. "They don't call me Casanova for nothing."

I laugh and climb off the bed. "They don't call you Casanova. I'll ask her at the funeral. A little gossip is good for the soul."

Joey deflates suddenly. His eyes grow bright. "We're burying her tomorrow," he says. "She's going into the ground."

It's like a water balloon in the face, a burst of cold, wet reality. I'm not ready for it yet. My body shivers. I've got to keep moving. "Come on. Let's go for a ride."

It takes Joey's mouth a second to switch tracks, but his hands are already reaching for the keys. "Where to?"

"You'll see."

The building is a low gray affair south of Colorado Boulevard that looks like an architect's representation of manic depression. The heavy block of metal and cement is highlighted by off-kilter windows with white sashes. They're supposed to make the place feel brighter on the inside. To me, it looks like a preschool for the criminally insane.

Dr. B's office is on the first floor, with a view of the parking lot.

Joey drops me off and keeps his questions to himself.

"I won't be long," I tell him. He waits in the car.

I knock on the first door on the right, and Dr. B calls

out that it's open. There is no waiting room here, just the hallway, and a dimly lit gray office with the mandatory guest chairs, walnut desk, and ficus tree in the corner. I drop into my customary seat at the far end of the lone couch.

Dr. B smiles and comes around the desk to take the chair opposite mine. She hasn't changed in the past year and a half—short black hair crisply cut into a bob, beige blouse and gray lady pants, the kind that have a matching jacket somewhere and come from a store that sells exclusively to women over forty.

"Jude," she says, and settles into her seat. "It's nice to see you again."

I laugh and shake my head. "Wouldn't it be nicer not to see me? Doesn't a visit signify some sort of relapse?"

Dr. B shrugs. "Not necessarily. There are preventative visits. And then there are the visits we do to satisfy our loved ones. Your mother, in this case. This is more of a checkup than anything else."

"Okay." I don't dislike the good doctor. Ever since she stopped trying to bullshit me. After three sessions of "you're safe here," she finally admitted bad things had to happen to good people, or she'd be out of a job.

"So, tell me about Maggie. I understand she was your best friend."

"Yes."

"And she killed herself." It's not a question.

"Reportedly."

"You have reason to doubt it?"

I like Dr. B, but I'm not sure I'm ready to tell all. So I shrug.

"When you were told it was suicide, how did it make you feel?"

Good old Dr. B. She's an ace at walking the middle path. She should have been a Buddhist.

That much, at least, I can share. "Like shit," I say.

"A classmate of mine committed suicide my first year of college," she says. Dr. B's pointless stories are meant to make it clear that you're not alone. But who's to say it's not just the two of you, then?

"I hear it's a stressful time."

"I didn't know him," she replies. "They held emergency meetings with the resident advisors and asked all of us how we felt. 'Like shit' would have been a good answer. I wish I'd thought of it at the time. Instead, I told the truth. I was annoyed. I was being coddled because some imbalanced kid killed himself in his dingy little dorm room. If they'd spent a little more time talking to him and less time talking to me, maybe he'd still be alive." Dr. B is tapping her pad with her pen now. She's looking through me, thinking back. "I wonder how you'll see all this in thirty years, Jude."

"Thirty years is an awfully long time," I reply.

"Yes, it is. But I'm here to tell you that it will all look exactly the same."

I shift in my seat and clear my throat. It's cool in the office, with the central air ghosting along silently, but I'm thirsty and the air is dry. "What do you mean?"

"That's what happens when people die. Time freezes around them. If you stand too close, you get caught, like a fly trapped in amber. It takes a certain amount of strength to pull away and leave it behind."

"This kid in college, you said you didn't know him."

She shrugs and leans back in her seat, intensity gone. "That's right. We had exactly one class together, a psych 101 symposium, ironically enough. There were two hundred and fifty of us in an auditorium every Monday for lectures." She chuckles. "You see, I even remember the day of the week. I remember looking him up in the roster after the news came down, hoping it would jar my memory of him, but it didn't.

"Of course, the difference here is he was a stranger. Maggie Kim was your best friend."

I feel a flutter in between my stomach and my chest. A sour taste hits the back of my tongue. "True," I concede.

She looks at me for a long time before saying, "So, I'll ask again: How does it make you feel?"

I'm caught in a middle place, unable to look at her, my vision gone heavy with unshed tears. I didn't think I'd ever be here again, in this room, with this woman and her questions. With this same drowning feeling inside.

When I speak, my voice is frogged and cracked. "She didn't do it."

"You're saying it was an accident?"

I clear my throat. "I'm saying Maggie had every reason to live."

Dr. B studies me quietly. This time, I hold her gaze. She jots a few more notes down.

"Plans for Christmas?" she asks, looking at her notes.

It's August. Summer suicides don't plan for the holidays. I tell her the truth. "Thinking about seeing my dad. Since it didn't work. This time."

She looks up from her notes and gives me a half smile. "So I heard. Good." She puts down her pen. "It's dry in here. Want some water?" She moves to the mini fridge behind her desk without waiting for an answer and hands me a bottle before swigging some herself.

"Tough room," I say, taking a pull from the bottle.

She smiles at me, and there's a twinkle in her eye. "I bet you say that to all your shrinks."

"Nope," I promise, holding my fingers in a scout's swear. "Just you."

Dr. B slides back behind her desk and opens the file cabinet, returning my folder to its proper place. "I'll tell your mom we talked. Don't kill yourself for the next ninety days, at least. It'll make me look bad." She winks at me. Unlike my mother, Dr. B knows when I'm a danger to myself. Lord knows she saw it, once upon a time.

"Good luck, Jude. If you ever want to talk, don't wait for your mom to call me."

I grab my bag and head for the door. "Oh, one thing," I say, stopping at the threshold.

"What's that?"

"Rohypnol. What's the clinical usage for it?"

Dr. B gives me a considering look. "Flunitrazepam. It's like Valium to the tenth degree. Technically, it's used for short-term insomnia and pre-surgical anesthesia. Easy to OD on it, especially with alcohol or opiates in the mix. Is that bit of trivia for you, or your friend?"

"Both," I say.

She looks at me for a long moment, and grabs a card from her desk.

"I want to see you again. When's the funeral?"

"Tomorrow."

"Okay." She writes a date and time on the card. "Friday, you and me, Jude. This talk was for your mom. Friday is for you."

I take the card slowly, and nod. Joey and Tallulah both said it straight. After tomorrow, I've got to find my way back to the land of the living. But not just yet.

"Flunitrazepam," I repeat. "Thanks, Dr. B."

To her credit, she doesn't ask the question that's clearly on her lips. "Watch yourself," she says. I shut the door softly behind me.

14

Roofies," I tell Joey when I climb back into his car. He closes the paperback he's been reading and shoves it beneath his seat. "*Cyrano*?"

He nods. It's the book he took back from Maggie. "You were saying?"

The sun sinks into the west in a blur of red and purple. The whole world is room temperature. It feels like we're indoors.

I shut the door and rock my head against the seat. "The roofies in Maggie's system. They're also called flunitrazepam. One of the drugs on Parker's list."

Joey stares at me and whistles low as it sinks in. "So she might have gotten the drugs from the house after all."

I nod. "Or someone did."

Mrs. Kim said Maggie was going to Hell. Who else had access to Parker's stash that might have helped her along?

"Violetta would have noticed the drugs missing," Joey says. He's right. Missing meds could cost her her job. She'd keep watch over something like that.

"One more thing to ask Violetta."

"*After* the funeral," Joey insists.

"After."

He nods, satisfied I won't make a scene in the middle of Maggie's service. "Where to next?"

"I don't care, as long as it's not here." I blink, long and slow, trying to soothe the headache that's starting behind my left eye. Maybe I should have let Shasta read my tarot cards. They'd have made more sense than all this.

Joey starts the engine and maneuvers us back onto the street. "This is Southern California," he says. "Let's go watch something burn."

We are not the only ones on the side of the road overlooking Angeles Crest. Families come out like crowds in a monster movie, early evening picnics in view of the fire line.

Dull orange light marches across the hillside less than

a mile away. As the sun fades, the firelight brightens, like the slow burn of a cigarette transforming leaves and paper into ash. The difference is, the families all head home eventually. Joey and I have nowhere we want to be.

We sit there in the turnout, our backs to the scenic overlook, watching the array of firemen and helicopters attempt to control the burn. It looks like Mother Nature is winning.

The sun is completely gone when we get back into the car and sit facing the lights of the city. Up above, the sky is gray bleeding into black, the smoke a pale miasma over the darkness. Stars fight to be seen over the streetlights and windows of the city. The air is oven-hot. A breeze moves toward us, not cool, but at least it's in motion. There's a music in the sounds of the city, the rush of the freeway, the rumble of trucks, the distant honking of horns and shouts down below. The fire helicopter hovers over the mountaintop, then buzzes away, a water-laden bumblebee. It's a lullaby of life, sung all day and night. I lean back into my seat and listen.

"Jude," Joey says. "If it turns out somebody did this to Maggie, what then?"

"Then we find them, and make them pay."

He hesitates. "And if it turns out it was an accident?"

I sigh and stretch, rolling out the ache in my shoulders. "Then I'm sorry I wasted your time."

"It's not wasted," he says. "It's just . . ."

"Just what?"

He shakes his head, and folds his hands behind his neck, eyes back on the night sky. "You're a hard girl to be around, Jude. This whole thing's been . . . hard."

I fold back in on myself, feeling threadbare, worn through. "I know," I tell him. "For you and me both."

A siren sounds in the distance, fading into the night.

Joey reaches to turn on his iPod, but I lean forward to stop him, my hand on his. For just that moment, we are so close, with his boy sweat and my own scent of exhaustion and sorrow.

Joey. He's always right here. I want to lean into him. I want to rest my cheek against his T-shirt and breathe him in, let him put his arm around me and tell me everything will be okay.

But I'm not in tears. This wouldn't be just mourning or comfort for a friend. What's safe for grief in the daytime is dangerous at night in a car with the top down and the city spread out before you. In the movies, it's expected. The girl cries and the boy comforts her with a kiss. This isn't a movie.

A hot wind blows across the arroyo. I blink, unmoving except for that slow scrape of lid over cornea and back.

A bare six inches between us, then four. I blink again, unable to breathe.

What would Maggie do? She would tilt her head back for a kiss. I can imagine the movement, so slight, so simple. An invitation. Joey couldn't help but lean in and kiss me, and then it would be done. Whatever came next would be a new maze to navigate, but not impossible.

Just tilt your head, I tell myself. Such a small move, from friend to female.

Maggie would have done it. She did it all the time, and made it look easy.

But I can't. I'm just not the tilting kind.

———————————————————

"What?" Maggie asked. It was September and we were lounging on a double-wide air mattress in the middle of the pool that would kill her by summer. Her hair was longer. Mine was exactly the same. "If it's not something Joey said, then what aren't you telling me?"

It was getting cloudy out and I was cold, but I didn't want to go inside just yet, so I sat there, forcing down the shiver rising inside me.

"I'm not telling you things I don't want you to know," I said.

"Is somebody hurting you?" She waited, knowing that I'd fill up the silence eventually.

I shook my head. It wasn't Joey. Sweet, normal Joey. He was my Mr. Almost. No, the real problem lay closer to home.

I wrapped my arms around myself, holding on to the warmth of my own body. "Roy tried to come into my bedroom last night."

"Son of a bitch," Maggie spat, grabbing my arm. "Your mom's boyfriend? Did he hurt you? Did he try to . . ."

I shook my head. "I locked him out."

"Did you tell your mom?"

I shrugged. "Not yet."

Maggie was livid. She almost flipped the raft sitting up in her anger. We wobbled and caught our balance. She laughed nervously and lay back down, curving her body toward mine.

"Why not, honey? She should kick the bum out. Jesus. Cut his balls off." She patted my arm, snuggling closer. "Too bad you guys don't have a pool house."

I looked at her, my heart racing faster. "Is that why you moved out here?"

She laughed. "No. I moved out so I could get laid without my brother listening in and smoke without freaking out my parents. And skip the hit parade every time there's a hospital stay. Remember?" She hung her head. "Shit. Just the opposite of you. And I'm no virgin."

It was my turn to sit up. I tucked my knees under my chin and looked down at my feet, deciding. "Well, neither am I."

Maggie dropped her glasses. "No shit?"

"No. Not since I was nine."

She sat up so fast I couldn't catch myself and we both flipped over into the deep end of the pool. Maggie sputtered to the surface and we paddled to the steps, hauling ourselves onto the deck.

"Another boyfriend?" she asked. "Another Roy?"

"Babysitter," I told her. "My parents were out celebrating their tenth anniversary. I asked to go, but they wanted some romance. Someone at my dad's office recommended a sitter and that was that. I ran, I tried to lock myself in the bathroom, but the lock kept slipping." I shrugged. "Bad locks. He didn't stick around afterward. Took off and left town."

"Did they ever catch him?"

I hunched in on myself, and it had nothing to do with

the cold. "Yeah. Trial, jail, the whole bit. But, it didn't change anything. My mom blamed my dad for hiring the guy. They split a year later." I chuckled. "I'm the only kid in history who really *is* to blame for my parents' divorce. So now Daddy lives in Vermont and we live out here."

"Do you ever see your dad?" Maggie asks.

"No. He's already got a replacement family. New wife. New daughter. New life. He keeps asking, though. Maybe next year. We've been talking about meeting up at my aunt's place in Jersey. It'd be better than being home all summer with Roy."

Maggie and I were wrapped in a towel together on the edge of the pool. The sun was out, clouds moved away, and I was no longer shivering. Instead, I'd started to talk, in a way I'd never done outside of Dr. Bilanjian's dim little office. In a way I couldn't do even then.

A grown woman could never truly understand what it's like for a nine-year-old girl to turn eleven and vomit in the backyard of a boy-girl party, terrified at the thought of spinning the bottle for her first kiss. For that same girl to turn fifteen and like a boy, even a really decent one, and not be able to touch him for fear of what might come next, of not being able to say no, or yes.

But Maggie understood.

She held my hand and let me tell her why I was still a virgin even though I wasn't anymore. She listened, and when I was done, she didn't tell me I was safe, that things would be okay. She didn't say how strong I was. Instead, she let out a long loud breath of air, like she'd been holding it the entire time.

She let go of my hand and pressed her palm to my cheek, looked me in the eye, and said, "Jude." She leaned in and rested her forehead against mine.

It was an intimacy that should have inspired terror, but it didn't. I was fixed in time. Like a photograph. She named me, and I felt whole.

The wind lapped at our towel and we pulled apart. Maggie sniffed and looked off across the yard, at the roses.

"My uncle felt me up once," she said. "My dad's older brother. Kissed me full on the lips when I turned thirteen and told me I was 'a woman now.'"

I rested my forehead on my arms, covering my eyes and blinking at the darkness. "What did you do?"

"Kicked him in the balls and told him he tasted like tuna." She started to laugh. "Which is even grosser now that I think of it. Then I told my parents. My dad didn't believe me, but my mom did. So now we only see good old Uncle Han on special family occasions. Weddings, funerals, and the like.

"Shit, it's getting cold," she said, although I was finally warm again. "Let's go inside."

We stood up and shuffled to the door of the pool house like two contestants in a sack race.

"My mom has no idea how much I love her for that," Maggie said, closing the door behind us. She stepped out of the towel and it slapped against me, cold and wet on my skin.

"Yeah," I said. "Your mom stepped up."

"So did yours," Maggie said, putting a kettle of water on the mini stove.

"Not really." I dropped the towel in exchange for a pair of sweatpants. "She didn't so much step up as run away."

"But she took you with her."

Only parts of me, I thought, and shrugged again, not knowing what else to say.

With a sigh, I push myself off the dashboard and back, deep into my bucket seat.

Joey lingers, still leaning forward, fingers playing over the iPod. Like he's waiting for me. The same hopeless way I've been waiting for Maggie.

But she's gone, and she's not coming back.

"I don't want to go home tonight," I tell him.

He looks at me. "Okay."

"Can we just drive?"

Joey nods and starts the car. The freeway runs like a river of light over the city. We make our way down the crest and curve north toward La Cañada. The San Gabriel Mountains rise up all around us and the night grows quiet and still.

At some point, I fall asleep.

I wake up in Joey's arms. He's snoring softly and doesn't resist when I pull away from him.

We're parked in front of his house. The sky is a deep purple, the shade it turns just before dawn. The street is empty, the houses silent and dark. It's as if the world has ended, lain down, and closed its eyes for good.

I should go. I should wake Joey up and send him to bed. I should call my mother so she doesn't worry. I should go home.

But I feel safe here. The two of us draped together in the dark, the stars beginning to fade from the sky. I fumble for my cell phone to check the time. Four a.m. and I've missed a slew of texts from my mother. She has to go to the office before the funeral begins, but she'll come back for me at 11:30.

I shut the phone and study the boy beside me. He looks peaceful. Eyes shut, lashes dark against his skin. I put his arms back around me, exploring the sensation, and watch him sleeping. And then I kiss him.

I kiss his lips and fall against him, and he holds me and comes awake saying my name. He pulls me in close and tight and it doesn't make me feel trapped.

No more running or building walls. Tonight, it sets me free.

In a little while, I'll leave him, I'll promise to meet him at the funeral. In a minute or two, he'll take me home and I'll go inside to my bedroom. I'll lock the door and wait until it's time to bury Maggie.

But for now, it's just me and Joey and the stars and the empty street and that warm, sweet kiss in the dark.

15

The day of the funeral dawns just as bright and hot as all the other days since Maggie died. I throw off my covers and lie there baking on my bed. The AC has given up the ghost again. Sweat plasters my tank and boxers to my skin.

A pressure in my chest keeps me pressed into the mattress, heat building behind my eyes, making them burn. It's only 7:00 a.m.

Joey dropped me off at sunrise and went back to get some sleep before the funeral. I must have dozed. A half-remembered dream evaporates into the stifling air before I can catch it, leaving room on my conscience for Maggie. And Joey.

I sit up and my mouth waters the way it does just before you throw up. I run to the bathroom, splash water on my face, and sit down on the closed toilet lid, breathing. In, out, in, out. Steady and slow.

The bathroom is cooler than my bedroom; the cracked and yellowed tiling keeps the room five degrees shy of the swelter in the hallway outside. But it's a small room, and it's closing in on me. I brush my teeth and skip the shower. It can wait a few hours.

Instead, I pull on yesterday's clothes, stuff my house key in my pocket, and slip out the back door. Inside, my mother's alarm clock goes off. Time for her to go to work.

Our neighborhood is awake, even at 7:00. Rusted pickup trucks pull up to start the morning gardening, lights come on in kitchens and bedrooms, kids running past the windows to their living rooms and morning doses of cartoons.

I walk the cracked sidewalks and watch the normalcy unfold at a distance. Maggie can't do this anymore. She can't wake up too early, can't go for a walk. She can't do anything but be buried, relegated to memory.

And suddenly, I remember my dream. Maggie's in the water and she's struggling, but somebody's holding her down. She stops fighting and goes under. Stays under.

Her killer looks up. And it's me.

I breathe deep, the smell of wet pavement and start-of-the-day lawn sprinklers. The snip of shears and soft thud of deadheaded roses from a nearby yard. I feel an emptiness in my chest and wonder if it's Maggie or Joey who put it there.

It's too early to go to a movie, or even the library. It's already close to ninety degrees and sweat drips down my nose as I walk. I hit Fair Oaks and turn into the strip mall on the corner, patting my pockets for enough money to buy a cup of coffee and a bagel. I find six dollars and stand in line at the coffee place, behind the suits and early-morning strollercizers.

I wonder if they can tell that I'm burying my friend today.

I think of the things Maggie knew about me, about Eppie and Dane. How everyone poured their hearts out to her. We only assumed she had done the same with us.

The thing I'm finally learning is that someone can be your best friend in the world, but you're not necessarily theirs.

I take a seat in the corner by the front window, away from the door. The glass is cool to the touch here, the industrial-strength air-conditioning working overtime. I search the morning faces to see if Keith is here again, but I don't see anyone I know.

I nurse an iced coffee, killing time until the house is empty. My mother wants to come with me to the funeral. Just a girl and her mom, lending her support. At least she's not farming me out to Dr. B this time.

I watch the line shuffling through the front door, watch people turn and gripe when someone holds it open too long. I try not to think about last night, but I wish Joey was here.

Kissing a friend changes things. I knew that when I left for the summer. I knew some things were better left undone. And right now I'm sick of change. Even Danielle with her face full of fried clams would be better than sitting here alone, waiting. Maybe I should have stayed at Joey's, or called Eppie or even Dr. B. But I didn't think I'd wake up feeling like this.

After the way this week's gone, I didn't think today would be even harder.

I sip my drink but ignore the toasted bagel beside it. I've got no appetite for breakfast just now.

Eventually, when the coffee is gone and the ice has turned to murky water, I throw my cup away, leave the bagel on the table, and head back out into the heat.

I walk up to the library with its green lawn and giant, shady trees. I take a seat on the roots of a spreading oak and watch dogs being walked, children wobbling on their bikes. I fall asleep in the shade, the sounds of traffic and summer playdates fading into silence.

No dreams or nightmares come. I wake up muzzy-headed and lost.

The park. The library. The funeral at noon.

I stand up, brush off my shorts, and walk home.

The house is empty when I unlock the back door. Another warm drizzle of a shower and I start to feel closer to human. I think about putting on makeup, but I'd just sweat it off. I settle for the natural grieving look and pull on my Jackie O outfit. What with chatting up Violetta, and burying my best friend, it's going to be another full day.

I hear my mother's car pull up outside. By the time I'm ready to go, she and Roy are waiting for me in the living room. My mom is wearing a black summer dress and has a straw hat resting on her knees. Roy is in jeans. Black jeans, to be specific, and a black button-down camp shirt.

I close my eyes and it's three months ago. Joey's waiting for me to close that gap between friend and girlfriend. And Roy starts wedging his way inside. I open my eyes. This is the universe's punishment for last night. This is what I get for trying on "normal."

"Ready, baby?" my mom says. "Roy's coming with us." She pats Roy on the knee and rises, hat clutched to her heart. "Don't you look nice? Roy, doesn't she?"

Roy rakes his eyes over me. "All grown-up," he says. I take a breath. And let it all out.

"Fuck you, Roy. Mom, he's not coming. Let's go."

My mother looks like a deer in the crosshairs. "What? Uh . . . Don't be . . ."

I raise an eyebrow and put my hands on my hips. "Don't be what? Ridiculous? Can't you *see* the way he looks at me? Or guess what he says to me when he knows you're not around? Open your eyes, Mom. Dust my doorknob for fingerprints. I'm sure you'll find a match. So, as I was saying, not him, not today."

"Baby," Roy says to my mother, seeing his free rent ticket hanging in the balance.

She doesn't look at him or at me. She stares down that tunnel to the past, the one with the regret-paved road running through it. She gulps the air, like she might cry. A second gulp follows, and a third.

"Royce Tremaine," she says, "when I first told you about . . . about *that*, it was in confidence. It was so you would understand me better, understand my *family*. I did not let you into this house lightly, and I sure as hell didn't give you carte blanche on my daughter."

She looks at him. Her eyes are fiery and rimmed with red. "Did you lay a finger on her?"

Roy has the courtesy to go pale. "N-no," he stutters.

"Did you?" My mother raises one of her fingers now and it is sharp as a knife, deadly as a gun. Roy pulls away, digging himself deeper into the sofa.

"We have good locks," I say, and my voice sounds smaller than I mean it to be. It's been a long time since I've seen my mother as a protector. I clear my throat and watch what it looks like, what it should have looked like years ago when the lock on my bathroom door wasn't as good.

My mother doesn't say anything else, though. She lowers her head and seems to crumble in on herself. "Okay, Roy. You're not coming."

Not. Coming.

My stomach plummets. If hope is a thing with feathers, then the last one's just been plucked.

Roy stands up, seeing the mama bear has no teeth. "I don't need this crap. These crazy . . . crazy accusations. I don't need it."

My mother shakes her head. "Let's go, baby," she says to me.

I start to laugh, ignoring the sting in my eyes. "Way to

show up, Mom. Way to give him a piece of your mind. For a minute there, I almost felt . . . safe. Thanks for that. Thank you for almost."

I leave them to each other in the overheated living room. I leave them to whatever it is two losers do when the blinders come off and the lights go up.

I wish I could call Joey for a ride. I need that now more than I ever needed that kiss. But you can't turn back time, so I walk to Fair Oaks and get a cab.

16

I'm late to my best friend's funeral. There's a joke in there somewhere, but I can't find it. The church is a monstrosity of 1950s design—a functional block of smooth peach-colored cement with a chalky white A-frame stuck in the middle, like the ghost of an IHOP restaurant that crash-landed on a warehouse store. A small brass cross at the peak of the IHOP lets you know it's a house of God. No wonder Maggie scoffed when her parents found religion. This place is hideous.

I mount the wide white steps, the heat reflecting off them in waves, and pull open the left side of the large gray double doors.

At least the inside looks more suitable for a funeral.

From here, the IHOP roof is revealed to be lined with tall windows. Sunlight pours down in rays that stripe the congregation below. Unfortunately, except for the pews and pulpit, peach and chalk is still the order of the day. Add in a crowd of black-clad mourners, and it looks like a set from an eighties movie.

Parker and his father are in the front row, Parker's wheelchair blocking part of the center aisle. Violetta is already sitting in the pew behind the family. Mr. Kim is talking to two people I can't see. His stance shifts and I'm surprised to discover Scott Dunfee standing before him, literally hat in hand, his brother Keith at his side.

Scott's in his dress uniform, all brass buttons and epaulettes. He's changed since the last time I saw him. Hardened, maybe. Grown older. He looks like a photo op standing there, jaw chiseled, eyes bright with emotion. Maggie would have swooned.

Keith is less striking, but he managed to dig up a blue suit. And I guess there is peace in the Dunfee family because Keith's got his arm around Scott's shoulders, shoring him up. Scott shakes Mr. Kim's hand. As if in silent agreement, the three of them move closer together and bow their heads.

Someone comes up behind me and I know it's Joey.

He's too close. A kissing distance. All I have to do is turn around. "Who are you looking at?" he murmurs into my hair.

"They're praying," I say, refusing to turn my head. I ignore the tingling in my back and focus on the curious sight of the jock and the hero, talking to God.

"It is a church," Joey replies. "Jude. Last night—" His fingertips brush my waist.

"Really, Joey? Now?"

He sighs and retreats a few inches.

I ignore him, unable to look away from that circle of grief on display.

Mr. Kim comes up for air and grips Scott's arm, wrinkling the perfect uniform. There is a stiff nod, a brusque pat on the back, and Keith leads Scott away to settle into a pew.

The viewing line shuffles forward.

"Are you ready for this?" Joey asks, his voice no longer intimate, but sad. His hand brushes mine, but I don't reach for him. "Jude?"

"Why wouldn't I be?" I'm going for bravado but, as I say it, the line of classmates and relatives shifts, and I see why he asked.

Hank was wrong about the casket. The Kims must've

hired the makeup artist to the dead stars, because Maggie Kim is lying in state, just the way she always wanted, black dress, pale skin, and a host of mourners lining up to say their final farewells. A blanket of red roses drapes the lower half of the coffin like an evening gown.

Just like that, I'm glad Joey's with me. I'm not sure I'd want to face this alone.

Mrs. Kim presses a hand to her daughter's casket. She allows herself to be led away, leaning heavily against none other than Edina Rodriguez.

Edina's traded in her YMCA swimsuit for a Maggie Kim costume—her dress is identical to the one in the coffin. I'm glad I didn't borrow it now. We would've looked like triplets. Her hair is pulled back into the tight Audrey Hepburn bun Maggie used to favor for formal dances. Maggie's pearl choker is back around Edina's neck. Just once, I wish the damned thing would live up to its name.

Edina sees me and Joey coming down the aisle. The look she gives me is no less than triumphant. She pats Mrs. Kim on the shoulder and goes back to playing the most aggrieved friend.

Joey and I follow the parade of mourners—Tallulah is there, Dane at her side, despite the traumatic breakup. The two of them look more like a *Vanity Fair* photo shoot than a couple of sad teens. I wonder if this is the start of a trend for them, a Catherine-and-Heathcliff affair that will leave them devastated, yet believing their love is inevitable. Maybe they just don't know how to be apart yet.

Like me and Maggie.

When she died, I let Joey take her place.

Behind them, Hank and Eppie have shucked off their wet suits long enough to pull on black outfits. They press their fingers, shaped into peace signs, to their lips and then to Maggie's forehead.

Joey and I move slowly forward.

A decrepit old man is being wheeled down the aisle in front of us, pushed by a young nurse. Maggie's grandfather or great-uncle, I can't remember. The other uncle, the one with the tuna breath, is off the guest list.

Then there's Parker. He doesn't approach the coffin, just sits there in his wheelchair. I wonder if he's already said his good-byes or if he's just sulking as usual.

One respectful row behind him, Violetta is looking not quite herself in a black dress and shawl. From my vantage point, I can see she is texting beneath her wrap. But with whom?

The thought passes as the old man is rolled away and Joey and I reach the casket.

Maggie. I start to say her name and stop. Margaret Kim, beloved daughter and sister, lies in the satin-lined box. I recognize her the way you would an old friend years later. Familiar, but strange. Someone you want to trust but can't because you don't know them anymore.

Margaret Kim is dead. But she's not my Maggie.

I sob in relief at the sight and Joey wraps an arm tight around me.

The body in this coffin is not the girl I knew. In those moments behind my eyelids—laughing at me from the side of the pool, couched next to me on the sofa in front of her old black-and-white movies—Maggie lives on. Sitting on my geometry homework. Waving at Luke through the telephoto lens.

She's still alive inside me.

I lean down and kiss her corpse good-bye, one cheek, then the next, pressing my lips into the pancake makeup inside the open casket. Its buttressed lid is the final proof that the cops are calling it an accidental death, and not a suicide after all. You shut the door on suicides. Accidents, on the other hand, are simply an act of God.

"You did it, babe," I tell her. "You made a beautiful corpse."

After a moment, Joey steers me back up the aisle, only

to be flagged down by Mrs. Kim in the front row. I bend down into her embrace, careful not to kiss her cheek so soon after kissing Maggie's.

"You will say something," she says into my ear. "When the minister says, you will speak." It's not a request.

I hesitate. Her arms hold me tight, as if she can make me agree by sheer force. A eulogy for Maggie. "Of course," I say.

If she'd asked me yesterday, like a normal person, I might have said no, or spent the night tossing and turning over what to say. But this is Maggie's mother, and that girl never took no for an answer. They're more alike than I would have guessed. Mrs. Kim nods, her hair brushing against my cheek, and releases me.

Joey is waiting. We return up the aisle and find seats in the sixth row.

A little while later the service begins. The minister goes on about unfairness, the prime of life, and God's great plan. I bow my head, but I'm not listening. I'm wondering where Lukey Loo is.

Then Joey nudges me. Maggie's father is taking the stage.

He looks dignified and drawn, as if he's aged ten years since yesterday. I wonder if it's taken this long for Maggie's death to finally sink in, or if it's a face he put on, the way his wife put on her makeup, to look the part of the grieving father. He buttons and unbuttons his suit coat nervously when he reaches the podium, and looks out across the audience with a weak smile.

"It's unnatural for parents to outlive a child," he begins. His voice is hoarse, but grows stronger as he speaks. "We've fought against it for years with our son, Parker. So, you can imagine, after so much diligence with one child, to have Death come along and steal the other, it's . . . unbearable."

He leans some of his weight on the podium, his breathing amplified by the microphone in front of him. There is a convincing amount of grief in his stance.

After a moment, he straightens. "Margaret Hye-Sun Kim was our only daughter. Intelligent, lovely and, admittedly, very independent. Too independent, a father might say." He laughs a little at this, giving the mourners permission to laugh with him. "We were proud of our daughter. Our little angel." He removes his glasses, wipes his eyes. "Thank you all for coming."

The whole room seems to be waiting, wondering what comes next.

I'm still chewing on the "angel" line when Joey nudges me again. "You're up," he says.

The minister is standing at the pulpit, watching me with a professional sympathy. I put my purse on the seat beside me and rise, a thousand drums playing inside my chest.

Heads turn. I feel eyes on me all the way up to the stage, my legs brushing against each other beneath the hem of my dress. I mount the three little steps, feeling the heat of all those eyes, and wrap my hands around the sides of the podium overlooking Maggie's coffin.

The last time I spoke in public, I was on the witness stand. The view is familiar, and so is the task. It's time to testify.

"Good afternoon." I clear my throat, wishing I'd brought a bottle of water. "For those of you who don't know me, my name is Jude. I was one of Maggie's friends."

In the audience, I see Edina squinting at me. Her eyes widen when I don't use the b-word, but "best friend" is hard to say when you have no idea why yours is dead.

"Maggie's parents asked me to speak today and, frankly, I didn't want to."

In the pews, people shift uncomfortably. Joey looks at his lap, then up again. I can feel him willing me to do my best.

"You see, Maggie was special. She could charm a squirrel out of a tree." I glance at Joey. He blushes. "She could look at the most unlikable person or the worst situation and find the good in it. In us."

Edina nods. Dane and Tallulah draw closer together. Eppie is crying on Hank's shoulder. Parker looks at his knees, shaking.

The hole is opening up beneath me again, the one that's been there every quiet moment, every night since Maggie died. I recognize it now, here, from behind the microphone.

I've fallen into this pit before. But Maggie pulled me out. This time, I'll have to climb out all on my own.

"So, I've been blaming myself for Maggie's death. I was out of town when it happened, and I keep thinking, whatever happened that night, maybe if I had been there, I could have done something to help." Heads nod in sympathy, or shake, expressing their own confusion. "But here, today, looking out across this room, I see family, friends, and classmates." Each group nods in acknowledgment as I scan the crowd. Edina and Tallulah hold their chins up. Stiff upper lip, I suppose. Or pride. "You all loved Maggie too."

There are murmurs of agreement. I clear my throat. "The difference is, all of *you* were here. And she's still dead."

Gasps. Edina scowls. Maggie's mother has a hand over

her mouth, her husband's arm around her. Parker is staring fixedly at nothing. Tallulah starts crying, Dane looks blank. Eppie and Hank are hunched together now, shoulders shaking. From tears, or laughter, I can't tell.

In the sixth row, Joey is shaking his head at me. *Make nice, for Christ's sake*, I can hear him saying. *It's a funeral after all.*

I take a deep breath and force myself to continue.

"So . . ." I pause and let the indignant mumbling die down. "So, now I'm thinking, maybe you can't save anyone. No matter how much we might care for someone, it's not always up to us. Could any of us have helped? Maybe. We'll never know."

Behind me, the cross on the wall creaks as the building shifts, a passing truck or a tiny earthquake making the foundation shudder. Temblors happen here all the time. There's just no way of knowing if it's an aftershock from some long-ago event, or a precursor of things to come.

I take another deep breath. Everyone is quiet now, not sure if I'm the enemy or just a kid who's hurting.

Frankly, I'm not so sure either. Because I'm realizing something, standing up here in front of Maggie's dearly beloved. The sort of thing that makes you feel like you're falling out of a Ferris wheel because it means there's no difference between holding on for dear life and letting go. Hold on and you'll eventually be crushed by the wheel; let go and gravity does the rest.

"We'll never know. But it doesn't matter," I say, "whether we could have helped or not. Because it's over. Maggie's gone. And now we have to let her go. Thank you."

I turn away from the podium and walk back down the steps, each one bringing me closer to the bereaved. Maggie's mother reaches out for me, eyes red, a real handkerchief in her hand. She pulls me into a hug and thanks me. Her father nods his head but says nothing. Parker's got his eyes on the middle distance. His jaw is clenched. Mine is too.

I make my way back to the pew where Joey is waiting. He pulls me into the seat like he's rescuing me, and maybe he is.

Maggie was my Ferris wheel. I can see that now. It was a ride with a view of everything I could never have found on my own. And now it's over.

I reach into my purse and pull on my sunglasses. That's enough sharing for today.

It's time to move on.

17

The service ends without further incident. There's an awkward reception in one of the peach-and-chalk-colored event rooms at the church. Everyone loves the brownies. Parker uses Violetta like garlic at a vampire ball to ward away the crowd. Something about a nurse and a wheelchair, people keep their distance. Joey gives me a nudge. I could force the issue, try to get her alone. But I find I've lost my appetite.

When we leave the church for the long drive to the cemetery, Maggie's mother detaches herself from Edina and wraps her arms around one of mine. "No, no, you ride with us." She tugs me down the wide flight of stairs to a waiting limousine.

"I don't want to intrude," I say. A glance tells me Edina very much wishes she could.

"Don't be absurd. You are family," Mrs. Kim says. I nod and tell Joey I'll see him at the grave site.

Violetta has just finished wrangling Parker into the backseat when I climb in.

"Ah. Welcome to the family, new sis," Parker greets me.

"Mom says I can have your room," I reply.

Mr. Kim scowls at his son, but it doesn't last long. "Now, children," he says, "let's all get along."

It's my turn to smile. Role playing is catching, I suppose.

We pull out into traffic behind the hearse. Through the tinted windows, I can see the blazing headlights of the cars behind us, glaring like cell phones held up at a concert, telling the world to step aside.

I look ahead to the hearse carving its way through traffic, black doors and chrome trim shining in the sun. I can just make out the top of Maggie's coffin and I wonder who feels colder, the girl inside that box, or me, trapped in my own padded crypt with her family. The AC blasts us from the front vents, drying sweat and the remnants of tears.

And I think religion got it wrong. Maybe Hell is a frozen tundra.

We ride in silence to the cemetery.

All my suspicions, my clever inquiries forgotten.

Maggie is gone and I couldn't save her. Now it's too late to try.

We bury Maggie at the Hollywood Forever Cemetery, just a few blocks south of Sunset Boulevard, in the heart of Hollywood. That, at least, makes sense. The graveyard holds the likes of Douglas Fairbanks, junior and senior, Vampira, and Cecil B. DeMille. Add to that a tradition of screening old movies for crowds of hipsters and cinephiles every summer, right up against the mausoleum wall, and I feel like Maggie's getting the kind of pajama party that lasts an eternity.

I wonder whose idea it was. I raise an eyebrow at Parker, but he looks away, staring out into the gritty streets where liquor stores and discount uniform warehouses vie for immigrant dollars in a clash of languages.

The park is beautiful. An oasis in the concrete jungle. A swan pond graces a stretch of green grass, and crypts rise up like temples to forgotten gods.

Maggie gets a strip of green across the road from the screening lawn, no trees or headstones to block the view. I keep my sunglasses on, and throw a rose on Maggie's coffin with the rest of the family. The Kims' gaggle of church friends is still droning hymns in Korean and English when I turn and walk away.

Joey finds me under the spread of a chestnut tree alongside the flat black road that winds through the park. Cars line the curb like gemstones in the sun. "How was that?" he asks.

I've convinced Mrs. Kim to let Joey drive me home. I've had enough of walking in Maggie's shoes for one day. I shake my head at Joey's question. "Let's get out of here."

"Not just yet," he says. I look up from the car door handle to see why. Luke Liu perches in a tree overlooking Maggie's open grave, using the limbs as a tripod. He's still taking her picture.

"Hey."

I turn around. Edina Rodriguez is standing there, looking more than a little uncomfortable. She glances at Joey, then back to me.

"Hello" is all I can think of to say.

Joey takes a step back. If Edina has something on her mind, it's for my ears alone.

"I didn't lie to you earlier," she says. "About the necklace. Maggie did give it to me." I notice it's not around her neck now. She's clutching it in her right hand.

"She said I could borrow it. Asked me to hold on to it, actually, for two weeks. She knew I loved it and lent it to me. Just for a little while." Edina is repeating herself, but I let her.

I look at the pearls in her hand, round and luminous. Her nails are bitten to the quick. "I've still got a week to go, but I don't want it anymore." She thrusts the necklace at me.

I take it, feeling the hardness of each little pearl. They're cool to the touch. A string of perfection.

Edina's eyes are red now. She blinks. "Poor Maggie." She looks up at me for comfort. I have none to give. "I . . . Poor Maggie," she says again, and after a moment's hesitation, she walks away.

"What was that about?" Joey asks, rejoining me.

I show him the pearls and put them in my clutch purse. "She claims Maggie asked her to hold on to them. Maybe she just doesn't want to be Little Maggie Kim anymore. It's no fun idolizing the dead."

Joey puts his arm around me. "Tell that to Marilyn Monroe."

"Is he coming down?" I ask, my eyes searching the branches for Luke.

As the last mourners depart, Luke lowers his camera

and waves at us. I see him fumble for his phone. A moment later, mine vibrates with a text.

Slides in. Be right there.

"Why didn't you call us?" I ask. I've kicked off my shoes and tucked my feet under my skirt. It's a bit too tight for me to curl up in a chair comfortably, but we've come to a coffeehouse rather than someone's home and I'm still in my Sunday best.

Luke blushes, pouring sugar packets into his iced green tea. "The developer called this morning. I knew you had to get ready for the funeral and I wasn't going to be missed if I came late, so . . ." He shrugs.

"You were missed," I say, and he blushes more deeply.

"I . . . I don't think I could have handled the service anyway."

"You couldn't have. They had an open casket after all," Joey tells him.

Luke pales, staring hard at the table. "How weird was that? I mean, dead people never look . . . right."

I turn my head and try to think of something sunny. Nobody speaks. Finally I clear my throat. "So, what've you got?"

Luke pulls an envelope out of his messenger bag. "I

had these printed from the slides. I haven't looked at them yet. I figured I should wait for you guys."

"Thanks."

He nods and unseals the envelope. A stack of 8 x 10 black-and-white glossies slides out onto the table.

"They should be chronological by time code," he says.

Joey and I are transfixed, the sharp photographs on the table erasing our last view of Maggie lying cold in a mahogany box.

I reach out and touch a photo. Maggie by the pool, blowing a ring of smoke. She looks so alive. The time stamp in the corner says she will be for another ninety minutes.

We sit there, letting Luke flip through image after image.

Maggie smoking, waving at him, calling him to her. Nothing we haven't seen before.

"That's when I went inside," Luke says. "And this is when I came out."

There are three photos left. Slow exposure. Dreamy. "I left the shutter open a long time to shoot by streetlamp," he explains. "I wanted to capture the moment."

The time stamp reads 10:35. 37. 40.

Three landscapes, forming a panoramic view of the yard after dark. The lamp in Maggie's pool house window glows like a fairy light, diffuse and unreal. The bright lights along the side of the house put the narrow walkway and the recycling bins in a pool of sharp focus. The rest of the house is dark. Everyone asleep except . . .

"Huh."

Luke sees it too. He leans forward.

"What?" Joey asks.

"There." He taps an upstairs window, at a point of light, no bigger than a Christmas-tree bulb.

"What's that?" Joey asks.

Luke shrugs. "Cigarette, most likely. See the way it's kind of dragging across the page, streaky?"

"Moving," Joey says with a nod. "I don't get it. Maggie never left the pool house and the Kims don't smoke."

"Maybe one of them does," I say. "When his nurse isn't on duty."

"What?" Luke asks.

I smile sadly. "Don't you recognize it? That's Parker's room. 'Resting calmly on anxiety meds by ten thirty p.m.,'" I quote Violetta's journal. "Ten minutes later, he's having a smoke. Twenty minutes after that, Maggie's dead."

Luke is crying silently. Joey hands him a napkin. "What, you think Parker saw something?"

I uncurl my legs from beneath me. "I'm betting on it."

Violetta lets us in. Today the AC is turned on, a chill hush that sends goose bumps up my arms and makes the house sound like it's sighing.

"The Kims are resting upstairs," she says. "Parker and I are out back for pool therapy." She turns, water dripping from her matronly swimsuit, despite the towel wrapped around her waist. She walks out to the pool without waiting to see what we do.

Joey and I exchange shrugs and follow her outside.

By the time we get there, Violetta is halfway down the pool steps, cradling Parker in her arms. He looks like a baby scarecrow, skinny legs curled up against Violetta's chest. His black swim trunks hit the water and cling to him, making him look even thinner. He catches sight of us and frowns.

"Returning to the scene of the crime?" I say.

"What do you want?" Parker snaps back.

"I want to know what happened to Maggie," I say. Sometimes honesty works.

Parker pushes away from Violetta, pulling himself to sit on a middle step, legs drifting in front of him, blue water lapping against his narrow chest. "She died," he says, squinting at me in the sunlight. I've got my shades on, as does Joey. So I let him squint up at us, knowing he can only see his own reflection in our lenses, weak and young.

"Is that so hard to understand?" he demands. "Maggie got drunk, got high, and she died."

"So it was an accident?" I ask, coming to crouch poolside.

He looks uncomfortable and shrugs, turning away. "How should I know?" he asks.

I reach into my purse and pull out Luke's photograph. I nod at the time stamp and point to the glowing ember. "You were, what, halfway through a cigarette? Had to open a window so your parents wouldn't smell it, right?"

"I don't smoke," Parker says. Violetta cuts him a look.

"So, this is someone else in your room at ten thirty at night?"

"That's private," Parker says. He looks very young.

Violetta wades over to look at the picture. "Smoking? Parker, how many times have I told you? Cigarettes will kill you."

Parker's shoulder's hunch. "It's not a cigarette. It was medicinal."

Joey and I exchange a look. "Medical marijuana?" I ask.

Parker shrugs and looks away.

Violetta relaxes. "That's right. That's the night we ran out of flunitrazepam and Valium."

I feel Joey come alert beside me.

Violetta prattles on, glad to have a break in her miserable day, I imagine. She laughs. "I swear those pharm guys are getting lazy, miscounting the order like that. I had to rewrite my log and everything," she says, shaking her head. "Sorry, Parker. You scared me for a second there. You can never be too careful with that stuff."

Parker keeps his eyes on the water.

"All right, that's enough PT for today," she tells him. "Do you want out?"

Parker doesn't respond.

"He just lost his sister. Talk to him," Violetta says to me. "Parker, *mijo*, it's good to have friends." The word falls flat in the still air, but she doesn't seem to notice. She makes sure he's settled on the steps, half in, half out of the water, and climbs out of the pool. "I'll be back," she says, and leaves the three of us alone.

The pool filter turns on, making a tinkling whirlpool of the water. Parker stares at the light dancing off the wavelets, reflecting in rings and stars on his skin.

"You watched her die," I say. "You gave her the drugs, then you smoked a joint and watched her die. Why?"

Parker shrugs, eyes still on the water that killed his sister. "What was I supposed to do?"

"Call for help. Get your parents!" A heat is rising in me. I push it back down. I want to understand.

"Did you know Maggie got into Brown?" Parker asks.

I take a deep breath. "I just found out."

"Yeah," Parker sighed. "She was going to tell you when you got back in town. Accepted a full year early. But no financial aid. Dad makes too much on paper."

I nod but don't say anything. Joey paces the deck behind me, looking up at the sun.

"I'm due for another surgery this fall. A hundred fifty grand, only twenty percent covered by insurance. Do you know how much it costs to go to Brown?"

I sit down, feeling sick. "About as much as an under-insured brain surgery?"

"Yeah." Parker hiccups and I see that he's crying. "What Violetta said about smoke killing me is true. The crap from all the wildfires is bad; cigarettes are worse. I started smoking because one good case of pneumonia in these shit lungs and I'd be off the surgery list, maybe even off life support."

"That's crazy," Joey says, not wanting to understand. But I do.

"Funerals are cheaper than treatment, Joe."

Joey looks at me, and I feel something inside me break.

That look on his face, I know it well: a kid who never knew the world could be so ugly.

I take his hand and try to draw him down to sit beside me. He pulls away.

"A lot cheaper," Parker says. "And Maggie knew it. She also knew it would kill my mom to lose me. But her?" He shrugs his thin shoulders. "Maybe not so much."

I take off my shoes and slip my feet into the water. It's cold, even on a hot day like today. I shiver until my legs get used to the idea.

Until I get used to the idea.

"She didn't call me."

Parker hangs his head. "She didn't want you to stop her."

"And Luke Liu?" I ask.

Parker looks at me with a pained smile. "She said he was her guardian angel. He couldn't be on duty if she was going to go through with it."

"So she slept with him, and sent him home . . ."

"I think she loved him . . . maybe," Parker says, as if hoping for that small comfort.

What a bitter pill, hope.

"Oh, Maggie," I sigh. Hating her. Hating Parker. "Did you know she gave Edina Rodriguez your grandmother's necklace?"

Parker sobs, a tear splashing onto his cheek. "For two

weeks. For safekeeping. She didn't want my mother to have to bury it with her."

Right. That was Maggie. Selfless, thoughtful Maggie.

Someone I barely knew. Someone I would never know now.

I feel the bile rise in me, feel the hurt, the stomach-clenching ache of loss and anger. For a moment, I'm glad she's dead. Glad I don't have to see her, to know how she lied to me. How she left a trail of confusion so I couldn't see the truth until it was too late.

They say suicide is a choice. Like the boy with the melting Popsicle versus the girl with the sunshine smile.

Maggie chose Parker over me.

The trouble is, she left us both behind.

"Why shouldn't I just push you into the deep end and let you drown?" I ask him, acid at the back of my throat. He's guilty after all, but it's survivor's guilt. He outlived Maggie. And that's unforgivable.

Parker shrugs. "I can swim, Jude. But if I couldn't, then Maggie would have died for nothing."

I laugh and shake my head. Wishing the murderous thought away.

Beside us, Joey sits, all but forgotten. He turns to Parker. "The cemetery. That was your idea?"

"No," Parker says wistfully. "That was all Maggie.

She and my folks bought that plot for me when I turned twelve. I wasn't doing so well, and Maggie said we could still watch movies together from the afterlife."

Joey blinks his eyes dry. "Are you going to tell your parents?"

Parker shakes his head. "What's the good in that? They'd never look at me the same way again without seeing her."

A bitterness fills my mouth that words won't wash away. "You mean the way they never saw her, only you?"

Parker hangs his head and a tear falls, rippling the water.

I can't blame him for being a coward. Lord knows I've been one too . . . with my mother, Roy, Joey . . .

We sit there for a while, the guilty and the guilt-ridden, turning browner in the hot Pasadena sun, pondering the point of it all.

But you should never question the dead. Their stance, by default, is inarguable.

Around us, the air roasts, filled with the ticking of air conditioners, the drip-drip of condensation, the warm-hay smell of dried palm trees and sunburnt pavement.

Maggie kills herself so her brother can live. And he lets it happen. Too afraid to stop her, too afraid to die.

Like there weren't a million other options in between. A million of them, and they all would have kept her alive.

But none of that matters now. Some decisions you can't unmake. Some harms can't be undone.

Maggie's suicide, Roy's lechery, Dane's infidelity. My rape.

All water under a very long bridge.

At last, I reach into my purse and pull out the strand of pearls. "Give these to your mother," I tell Parker, and drop them on the deck of the pool. I rise to my feet. "I'm going home."

"God, I can't wait to get out of this place and go to college."

Maggie and I were poolside yet again, at the start of our junior year, propped up on our elbows, toes dangling in the water.

Up at the main house, the cavalcade of concerned friends was making an appearance. Parker was home from the hospital. Not a surgery this time, just observation after a bad fever. In honor of his return, Maggie was smoking her nasty filterless cigarettes and blowing the smoke toward the house.

"One more year after this one," I reminded her. The future, as they say, was wide open.

"Do you know where you want to go?" she asked me.

I laughed. "Who cares, as long as it's not here?"

"You surprise me," she said. "I always took you for an Oxy girl."

"Guess again." Going to school within five miles of home, even to Occidental, was out of the question. "Besides, you're going back east. Wouldn't you miss me?"

Maggie sighed and leaned back on her lounge chair, taking a luxuriant drag from her smoke. "Darling," she said after she inhaled, "I'll miss all the little people. Do you hear me?" She sat up suddenly, sunglasses glinting in the afternoon light. "Darling"—she blew me a theatrical kiss—"I'll miss you all!"

18

"I'll take you home," Joey says, jogging after me through the Kims' side gate and onto the street.

I turn around to face him. "No, Joe. Not this time."

His face creases. "Jude? What's going on?"

I take a step toward him. In my heels, I come level to his chin. I put a hand on his right cheek and kiss him on the other. "Thank you. For being with me through all this. You can go now. I'll be all right."

But Joey doesn't leave. He looks down at me and puts his arms around my shoulders. He doesn't pull me to him. That's a distance I'll have to close myself.

"Well, maybe *I'm* not all right," he says. "Did you ever think of that? Maybe I need you here with me."

I can't look him in the eye. I needed Maggie, not the other way around. I don't want to do the same thing to Joey. Not if there's a choice.

"You don't deserve a train wreck like me, Joey. Find a girl who knows how to love you the right way."

His arms fall away like dead leaves in autumn. "You mean a kid, like Amanda Liu?"

I think of Luke's little sister, young and naïve, untouched by all this bitterness. "Yes. Like her. You're a good guy, Joey. You deserve a little innocence."

Joey seems to cave in on himself, shoulders collapsing like a scarecrow without its straw. After a moment, he steps forward and presses a kiss to my forehead.

I can feel the sorrow in it. The pain.

"I guess it didn't work, then," he says when he steps back.

"What didn't?"

"Being there for you. Being good."

Something shifts in my chest. That hollowness from this morning that I thought was because of Maggie. It was Joey all along.

I feel it like a physical pain. The sound of a heart trying to beat again. Trying and falling short.

"Almost," I tell him. "It almost did."

Joey makes a study of the sidewalk, cracked and

wavering in the heat. With a little shrug, he pulls himself upright and reaches into his shirt pocket. "Here."

I hesitate, staring at the photograph in his hand: a little girl, nine years old, wearing a sundress and a smile as big as the sky.

Me. The way I used to be.

My throat tightens. "That was Maggie's."

"It was stuck between the pages of my book."

That dog-eared copy of *Cyrano* sitting on his dashboard. The one he's been driving around with all week. I'd thought it was a reminder of Maggie, of their friendship. I guess I was wrong.

And just like that, it falls into place. The last piece of the puzzle. Maggie knew what she was doing the night she died. She had always known.

The pearls given to comfort Edina, held in trust for her mother.

Seducing Luke Liu.

Sending me three thousand miles away.

Making plans to hang out with Joey so he'd be the one to find her. Knowing how I would turn to him.

Every one of her affairs had been put in order. Including mine. The right picture in the right hands at the right moment.

Maggie Kim's bequest to me. A chance to be happy again.

All I have to do is reach out and take it.

Joey is looking at me, trying to see that little girl in the person standing before him, the way Maggie wanted him to see her. The way only she ever saw me.

But that little girl's not here anymore.

And that's what I loved about Maggie. She had hope for me, even though it was lost.

"It's a nice picture," Joey says.

"I know." I reach for the print with cold fingers.

Joey starts to say something and, for a moment, we are both tethered to the photograph of the little girl with the impossible smile. The one Edina had called "happy." It trembles between our fingers.

And then he lets it go.

I take a deep breath.

"I want to go home, Joey."

He kisses me on the forehead again, releasing me.

"Then go."

I hear his shoes scrape the sidewalk, the buzz of a passing plane, the click of the air-conditioning units struggling up and down the block. He starts his car and I could stop him, tell him I was wrong, tell him I want to give us a try.

But I'm not that girl. Not even Maggie could change that.

When he drives away, I don't look back.

19

There's unexpected furniture on the little patch of dead earth we call a front lawn. Not much. A folding chair, some TV trays, a portable radio, littering the yellow grass like the end of a yard sale. I recognize it all as Roy's.

I kick off my shoes coming up the walk and enter the house through the front door.

The living room is empty. Music is playing in my mother's room. The door is shut.

I pass through the house. The kitchen is spotless, and the bath mats have been washed and hung over the bathroom shower rod to dry.

It's my mother's post-partum ritual. When something ends, you clean house and wait for the next thing to begin.

When I was born, my father said, she even polished the silverware.

I go to my room and change out of my black dress and fake pearls. It feels like a costume coming off, like a layer of pretense being torn away. I'd shower if the bath mats weren't hanging. Instead, I go into the bathroom and wash my face.

In the mirror, I look twelve years old again. The denim shorts and faded T-shirt remind me of summers back east, when there were three of us in my family. When family was more than just a word.

I turn away from the mirror and go sit outside.

On the front steps, I watch Roy's belongings become a part of the landscape, and wonder if my mother kicked him out, or begged him to stay. And how long it'll be before he, or some opportunistic Dumpster diver, comes along to claim his junk.

A warm breeze rustles across the grass, bringing the scent of baked hay and ash.

I'm still sitting there when the music stops and my mother comes out to join me.

"Roy's gone," she says by way of greeting. My mother looks different when she's single. Cleaner, somehow. Whole-grain bread instead of brioche.

"Good riddance," I say.

"It's just you and me now."

We sit for a moment in silence, watching the grass die in the heat of the sun. "I'm so sorry about Maggie," she says. "And about Roy."

I take a deep breath and let her have her piece.

"I didn't see it, or I'd have stopped it," she promises.

I could say the same about Maggie's suicide. I would have stopped it, but I chose not to see.

"I want you to know," she tells me, "I'm going to keep trying. I want to be a better mother to you."

The way I want to be a better daughter, a better girl-friend. A better friend.

"Sure," I say. "You'll try. I'll try. We'll all try." It's a familiar tune. I dance the steps without even counting. Because some of us don't get second chances.

It's my mother's turn to sigh, and she does so, exhaust-edly. "Why do you blame me for everything?" she asks in a thin, weary voice.

"Not everything, Mom. Just the one thing. Isn't that enough?" I don't know why I say it. I can lay blame at my mother's feet, at my father's. At Maggie's, at Parker's. At mine. But I'm angry, and she's an old familiar target for the blow.

This cues her exit. Every time, my mother stands up, looks out into the middle distance, and walks away. But not today.

Maybe because a girl my age is dead, someone my mother knew. Someone I loved.

Maybe because it's a Thursday and the yard is full of trash.

But she doesn't leave. She just leans back with her elbows on the top step, her back wedged against the cracked concrete between the bottom and middle stair. "I wonder," she says. "I wonder if you'll ever forgive me for not protecting you."

It's a new note in the old song, and for once, I have to think of my line. "That depends," I say.

"On what?"

"On whether or not I can forgive myself."

One dark night long ago, a bad man did a bad thing to a little girl who's been bad inside ever since. Nobody saved me the way Maggie tried to save her family.

Even I fought for my friend more than I ever fought for that little girl. Maggie meant the world to me. Why should I be worth any less?

I feel that Ferris wheel again, and I'm tumbling out of it, fingers slipping, wondering if I can let it all go.

Then the record skips and gets back on course.

"You were just a kid, hon," my mother says. "Just a child."

"I know."

We're all just little kids in the big wide world. Making choices every day. Right or wrong. Skinning our knees and getting back up again until the day we simply cannot rise.

I pull the photograph from my pocket and give it to her. The last picture of her innocent little girl.

My mother gasps, staring at the photo in her hands. I can feel her heartache, homesick for that child's smile.

She puts an arm around me, and I let her pull me into a small half hug.

We sit on the steps, our shoulders pressed together, her head leaning against mine. I can feel it through my bones when she echoes my words. "Yeah," she says. "You know."

August in Pasadena. Fire, heat, and ash as the Santa Ana winds blow out of the west, scouring the dead fronds from palm trees, igniting the manzanita and chaparral. It's the song of Southern California, fire, mud, and earthquake; tear it down, build it up.

The earth shakes, the houses burn, and people die, damned and unforgiven, or saved. But the rest of us remain.

Maggie Kim is gone.

I'm the one who must endure.

ACKNOWLEDGMENTS

A book has many midwives and *Pasadena* is no exception. Many thanks: To Rahna Reiko Rizzuto—the first person to read what I thought was my "perfect" fifty-page draft and tell me that it could be more. To the amazing Evie Lindbloom, whose librarian superpowers helped me understand the details behind Maggie's demise. To Kirby Kim, my agent, who saw beauty in the book and championed it. To my editor, Shauna Rossano, who stuck by the story even while starting her new family. To Katherine Perkins, who rode shotgun while Shauna was creating a masterpiece of her own. To Danielle Calotta, who gave the book its amazing cover, one that captures the smudged glamour of Southern California perfectly. To the soul of Raymond Chandler and all of the great noir storytellers of film and page who drew shadows out of sunshine and studied the darker side of the human condition. To Hedgebrook writing retreat for giving me shelter while I breathed more life into those first fifty pages. To the beautiful city of Pasadena for being an inspiration. And especially to my husband, Kelvin. This book is for him. Without his love of noir, I would have never attempted it in the first place.

Thank you, one and all.